THE CURVY GIRL CLUB

ALL GROWN UP

KELSIE STELTING

Copyright © 2023 by Kelsie Stelting

All rights reserved.

No part of this book may be reproduced in any form or by any electronic or mechanical means, including information storage and retrieval systems, without written permission from the author, except for the use of brief quotations in a book review.

This is a work of fiction. Names, characters, businesses, places, events, locales, and incidents are either the products of the author's imagination or used in a fictitious manner. Any resemblance to actual persons, living or dead, or actual events is purely coincidental.

For questions, address kelsie@kelsiestelting.com.

Editing by Tricia Harden

Cover design by Najla Qamber Designs

Readers sensitive to certain types of content should visit kelsiestelting.com/sensitive-content to learn more.

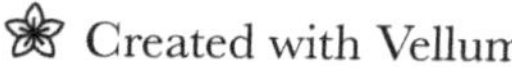 Created with Vellum

For anyone who's ever felt alone.
Welcome home.

CONTENTS

1.	Rory	1
2.	Callie	10
3.	Jordan	19
4.	Ginger	25
5.	Zara	35
6.	Rory	43
7.	Callie	53
8.	Jordan	63
9.	Ginger	77
10.	Zara	89
11.	Rory	96
12.	Callie	106
13.	Jordan	116
14.	Ginger	126
15.	Zara	136
16.	Rory	148
17.	Callie	158
18.	Jordan	167
19.	Cori	174
20.	Ginger	176
21.	Zara	188
22.	Rory	191
23.	Carson	195
24.	Callie	202
25.	Jordan	207
26.	Ginger	212
27.	Ray	218
28.	Zara	225

29. Rory   233
30. Beckett   242
31. Callie   248
32. Jordan   254
33. Ginger   259
34. Zara   263
    Epilogue   267

    Bonus content!   273
    Author's Note   275
    Also by Kelsie Stelting   279
    Acknowledgments   281
    Glossary   283
    About the Author   287

ONE

RORY

I STARED at the pregnancy test on the counter, praying for two pink lines to appear. The strip slowly saturated, and the control line turned pink. I crossed my fingers on both hands, hoping with everything I had that this would be my month. This would be the month our family truly began.

I didn't see a second line at first, but I knew the directions well enough to know that even the faintest of lines meant pregnant. A little flicker of hope held out as I lifted the test up close to my eyes, hoping there was something I'd missed. Something that I hadn't caught at first.

But all that stared back at me was... nothing.

With tears stinging my eyes, I threw the test in the trash, one of dozens to hit that trash can in the last year and a half of trying and failing and trying again, only to reach the end of the month and feel like my body had betrayed me. Betrayed us.

Beckett was still getting dressed in the bedroom, getting ready to leave on a work trip that would keep him away for a few days, and I'd wanted so badly to give him good news. Something that would make him want to rush home.

Instead, he got me.

I stared in the mirror, wishing I didn't have this desire, this need to have a family. Instead, I saw red-rimmed eyes, PCOS acne, and the knowledge that there was no life growing inside me.

I put on my makeup, trying to get ready for the day through the pain that hollowed out my chest every month. It was a cruel joke, being an art teacher and working with children day after day when you couldn't have any of your own.

Then I slipped into the stretchy dress pants that were great for moving around and a flowy blouse I wouldn't mind getting paint on. With nothing left to do, I stepped out of the en suite bathroom.

My husband stood beside the bed, placing clothes into his travel bag stamped with the Brentwood Badgers logo. He was handsome when we started dating senior year, but he was even better looking now, with his brown hair cropped just long enough to be messy. His eyelashes unfairly dark and long. His jaw strong, clean-shaven. He'd gone from a boy to man in every way, and I'd gotten to experience it all with him.

That conventional wisdom was right when it said to marry your best friend. We were coming up on three years of marriage next month, and in so many ways, it had been the best three years of my life. The only thing that could have made it better was having a little Beckett running around our home. Getting to see the way Beckett loved a child of our own like he did our nine-month-old nephew.

Aiden, my brother, and his wife Casey's baby had been a surprise in their last year of college. Casey gave birth a month after graduating, but their family, their child, was perfect in every way.

Beckett glanced up from his bag, a hopeful look in his hazel eyes, and it took all I had not to break down in tears all over again. Unable to speak, I only shook my head, and he took me in his arms, holding me close.

"I'm sorry," I cried, the dam fully breaking.

"It's okay," he breathed, stroking my hair as he held me. "It's just not our time yet. A baby will come. I promise."

I didn't know if I believed him. I'd been so excited to try for a family after I landed a job teaching art at our old school, Emerson Academy. With both of us having good jobs—him as the official photographer for the local professional football team and me as a teacher—there was nothing holding us back... except me.

He drew back, keeping his hands on my shoulders and looking me in the eye. "Hey, remember what you said in your vows?"

I nodded slowly. "'It's always you and me against the world.'"

He smiled gently, then pressed a kiss to my lips. "Just as true today as it was then."

I nodded, wanting to change the subject. "About ready for your trip?"

"Yeah, but I left my flash at the office."

"Shoot," I said, turning to the closet and looking for the socks my students loved. They were pink with paint brushes and palettes all over.

"Are you sure you don't want to fly to Pittsburgh after school lets out and hang out with me before the game?"

I pulled the socks out and turned to him. "I promised Aiden and Casey I'd help them with a mural in Casen's room this weekend."

Concern crossed his hazel eyes. They captivated me just as much now as they always had. "Are you sure you're up for it, considering..." He gestured toward the bathroom.

"It'll be good," I lied. I lifted my lips slightly to make it more convincing. "Plus, maybe holding Casen for a little while will make my arms feel less empty."

Beckett pressed his hand to my cheek. "Call me, text me, whenever, okay? I'm here for you."

I took his hand and kissed the inside of his palm. Even though *The Kissing Hand* was technically a children's book, I liked thinking my love would go with him wherever he went. "I love you, Beckett Langley."

"I love you, Rory Langley."

My smile was genuine this time. The sound of my name on his lips never got old.

He zipped his bag closed and put the strap over his shoulder. "I'll be back Wednesday morning. Can you get off for lunch? I can bring over some takeout and eat with you."

I nodded. "I can swap lunch duty with Mom."

"Perfect." He kissed my cheek, then left.

But being alone in our home felt so much lonelier than ever before. We had a beautiful three-bedroom house that we'd decorated room by room, painting the walls with murals and hanging pieces of art we held dear. But the negative pregnancy test in the bathroom trash can was all I could think of.

Unable to ignore it, I got a plastic bag and put the test inside, then left for school, bringing it with me.

Since teachers had to get there early, the parking lot was pretty much empty, but my mom's car was among the vehicles already there. I went to the high school building, where I worked in the mornings, and went directly to her classroom.

She had her head bent over the desk, focusing on papers, but I put the pregnancy test down in front of her.

She looked from me to the test, and the hope in her eyes almost gutted me. But when she looked closer, she frowned. "Negative again? Are you sure you were testing your temperature at the right time to track your ovulation? Maybe it's time to go by cervical mucus instead?"

I frowned. "I'm certain I ovulated this month. What I want to know is why you always made getting pregnant seem so easy in health class! You made it sound like the first time I looked at a guy, he'd have eye-sex with me and plant a baby in there!" I gestured at my stomach.

"The curriculum definitely leans more toward pregnancy prevention for high schoolers, Rory, not family planning." She was trying to be gentle, I could tell, but Mom was straightforward, as usual. "We didn't exactly want you all tracking your cycles and getting pregnant on purpose."

I rolled my eyes. "And of course, it was easy for Aiden and Casey. They probably did the whole eye-sex thing."

Mom laughed. "You're probably right. And they suffered plenty for it. Casey had to drop out of the track team that last year. Their student loans are so high now."

I didn't want to say it, but I'd pay triple the loans I had if it meant I'd have a baby in my arms.

"You've done everything right," Mom said, taking the test and putting it in the trash can beside her desk. "The metformin helped with your insulin resistance. You've been going to yoga after school to manage your stress. You're ovulating. It will happen for you, honey. I know it."

My heart ached painfully. "We've been trying so long; it just seems hopeless."

"Maybe it's time to try Clomid?"

I nodded, playing with the edges of my shirt. Beckett and I weren't crazy about Clomid and the possibility of multiples, knowing it would be so much for us to handle at once, but maybe we could talk about it when he got back.

"You know what you need?" Mom said. "A girls' weekend to get away and forget it all for a little while. Maybe you can get the old crew together... Isn't Callie living in a vacation spot now?"

I laughed slightly. "I'd hardly call central North Carolina a vacation spot, but maybe we can meet at Myrtle Beach. If Jordan ever has any time off school."

"Great idea," Mom said. She looked behind me and said, "Hi, Belinda! Can I help you?"

I turned and smiled at the girl. She was one of the best students in the senior class. "Hey, girl, hey," I said to her, smiling. Then I waved to Mom. "See you later."

I got out my phone as I walked to my classroom and sent a text to the Curvy Girl Club group chat. It had been a couple weeks since we'd texted, with everyone so wrapped up in their jobs and relationships.

I wanted to change that. I missed them so freaking much, missed the days when we met at

Zara's locker to talk in the morning and went to Waldo's Diner for milkshakes after a football game.

So I sent a text.

Rory: Anyone up for a group chat tonight?

Zara was the first to reply.

Zara: As long as it involves margaritas.

TWO
CALLIE

I WAS HIDING in a dark closet at work, crying my eyes out for the third time this week and wondering how I was going to pull myself out of here. Being a social worker was nothing like I imagined. I was completely overwhelmed all the time, rarely felt like I was making a difference, and regularly on the verge of tears.

I'd thought working in foster care would mean helping kids who grew up like Carson, but the reality was so much bleaker. Sure, there were some children who got placed with great families, or birth parents who stepped up to the plate and made changes for their kids, but that happily ever after was the exception, not the rule. At least from what

I'd experienced in the last couple of years working for the state.

The best part of my days was always going home, meeting Carson at the HOA gym where he worked, then swimming for half an hour, eating dinner, and falling asleep. The weekends were better, as we typically spent them with Carson's sister Clary's family, but we didn't really have any friends here. North Carolina still didn't feel like home.

Not like Emerson.

I pulled out my phone to look at my friends' social media, but my phone lit up with a text. I let out a quiet, tearful laugh, so thankful there was a new text in the Curvy Girl Club group chat.

I opened the text messages, wiping my eyes so I could properly read the words.

Rory: Anyone up for a group chat tonight?

Zara: As long as it involves margaritas.

Jordan: I think I can take a quick break in the supply closet.

I let out a humorless laugh. Jordan and I were cut from the same cloth that way. We both had to sneak away to closets to get time for ourselves. I hesitated before replying. I'd been avoiding my friends and even phone calls with my mom, trying to make it work here, to force myself to get out and make new friends. But it wasn't happening. And I missed Emerson like crazy.

Ginger: I'd love to! What time were you thinking? I'll make sure I'm in service.

Rory: I don't know. Callie? Are you free?

I looked at my name, my eyes blurring over again. Why had I stayed away from them for so long? Why had I stayed away from Emerson? Sure, flights were expensive, and Carson and I were on a tight budget, but my parents gladly would fly me home if I asked them to...

Callie: I'd love to talk. Set a time and I'll be there.

Rory: Five work for everyone?

There was a quick round of replies, and we landed on 5:15. It was the most exciting news of my day.

I wiped off my face before getting up and going back to work. I had paperwork and a couple of home visits to do before I could call it a day.

The hope of a video call was the only thing that kept me going. Which was probably a good sign I should quit. That was all I could think about as I drove through rush hour traffic to the gym.

Carson greeted me outside, like he always did, a big grin on his face. His hair was shorter now than when we were teenagers, but his grin always took me back. It was so happy and melted my heart, just like it had all those years ago.

I turned off my car and lifted my fingers in a wave. My heart felt heavy. Everything about me felt heavy. All the stress from my job had caused me to gain almost thirty pounds in the last couple years, even with a regular exercise routine.

"Hey, baby," he called, walking toward me. He looked so good in his workout clothes, his arm muscles showing off in his sleeveless shirt.

"Hey," I said, leaning into his hug.

He held me tight. "Another hard day?"

I nodded, fat tears rolling down my cheeks. "I had to bring that boy back home. I could hear them yelling before I left." My shoulders shook with sobs. "He deserves everything, and he's getting..." *Exactly the kind of life you got,* I couldn't say.

Carson cradled my head, holding me to his chest, right there in the parking lot. I was worried about embarrassing him at his work, but he didn't seem to care, riding out my sobs with slow and steady breaths. "Babe, you've got to leave this job. It's tearing you apart."

I sniffed, looking up at him. "I thought if I hung in there, if I made relationships with the judge and my supervisor, it would make a difference, but it's not. I can't save those kids. And being there for them, getting to do a worker visit once a month, it's not enough. And I don't even have enough time to foster dogs anymore. So I'm failing these kids, and I'm failing animals, and I can't give you all of me because it's all gone at the end of the day. I'm failing at everything that ever mattered to me." I took a breath after letting it all out. "This isn't what I wanted for my life. I should have stuck with the plan and gone to vet school instead of thinking I could be some sort of savior."

He cradled my face in both of his hands, his ocean-blue eyes a pool of safety and love and none of the hatred I was feeling for myself. "Quit your job." He'd been telling me this every day for months... and maybe it was time for me to listen.

I nodded. "I'll find a different job. I don't care if I have to wait tables."

He shook his head. "No, you need to heal, Cal. I don't care how long it takes, if we need to put things on a credit card for a while..."

"I can't do that to you," I said, my heart breaking right along with my voice. "You've already given so much, Cars."

"I'd do anything for you." He kissed my forehead. "Anything to stop seeing you like this every night."

I nodded. "I'll quit." The second the words were out, I already felt relief wash over me. He was right. I had to know when to call it quits. It was long overdue.

"Can you put in your your resignation tomorrow?" he asked. "I don't want you going in and trying to stick it out until a better time comes around."

I nodded, and he put his arm around my shoulder, walking toward the gym doors with me.

Now that we'd decided, in just that short conversation, I felt a weight lifting from my shoulders. Like now I could let go of survival mode, even if it took time.

"I know this sounds crazy," I said, "but working at a restaurant actually does sound kind of nice. People ask me what they want, I get it for them, they eat and they're happy. At least for a little bit. And if someone messes up, it's as easy as making another plate."

Carson chuckled. "Gayle and Chris always did make running Seaton Bakery look like so much fun."

Fun. A word I'd hardly thought of in the last

year. "Speaking of fun, I'm doing a call with the girls tonight."

His grin was wide. "That's great. You need to be in touch with them more often."

"You're one to talk. When's the last time you and Beckett spoke?"

"Actually, we were on the phone this morning. He called and invited us to watch the game in Philly."

My mouth fell open. "A Steelers game?"

Carson nodded. "He has a couple tickets since Rory didn't want to go... It sounds like she's having kind of a rough time."

I frowned, feeling bad for Rory and feeling like an even worse friend for avoiding her and the others. "What's going on?"

"Don't tell her I told you, but they're trying for a baby, and it's not going so well."

"Ugh, that's awful." My heart broke for her. "She would be such an amazing mom." We stopped outside the locker room doors, about to go our separate ways through to the pool.

"I know," he agreed. "If I could think of the two best people to be parents, it's them... or us."

My eyebrows rose as I looked up at him. "Ten years from now, right?"

"I don't know..." He shrugged. "It doesn't sound that bad. And with Joe and Gemma having a kid on the way... I'd like for our kid to have cousins to play with that are actually their age."

I was so not expecting this. "I thought you didn't want to have kids until we had a house."

He shrugged again. "One guy who goes to the gym here is a real estate agent. He said there are grants for first-time home buyers that could cut our down payment way back... to something we could actually manage."

"Not if I quit my job," I said. "Our last car repair wiped out most of our savings."

"But a mortgage would be cheaper than rent," he returned.

He had a point. "It's a lot to think about," I said. "Quitting my job, buying a house, having kids..."

"You always said you'd want to be a stay-at-home mom like yours... Maybe each stumble at work has led us closer to here. You know exactly how you want a kid to be treated, and I know with your big heart, you could give them more than enough. Besides, putting a baby in you would be awfully fun." He grinned.

I reached out and hit his chest.

He pretended like it hurt.

I smiled and laced my fingers through his. "You really would be the best dad, Carson. I've always thought that. Especially to a little girl."

He grinned back at me, tucking a lock of hair behind my ear. "I'm not saying we have to get pregnant today or tomorrow or even six months from now. Just think about it, okay?"

"Okay," I said.

We pushed into our separate locker rooms, and I changed into my swimsuit, thinking about life after quitting my job. Life as the kind of wife Carson deserved, who could be the rock for him too from time to time. Life as the stay-at-home mom I'd always dreamed of being.

"JUST A FEW STITCHES LEFT," I said to the older man who'd had an accident in the garden, cutting himself on an upturned rake. I slid the needle carefully through his skin, making precise stitches to hold the wound together. After tying off the thread, I cut it with a pair of scissors and said, "Got you all sewed up! Take a look. Now, you can wash this with soap and water, and make an appointment with your regular doctor in two weeks to have the stitches removed, okay?"

He nodded, straightening the Heywood Co-op hat on his head. "Will do, Ms. Jordan."

I smiled, standing with him. "Have a good day, Mr. Fredericks."

I was so happy when they gave me a clinical

rotation was in Heywood. It was a smaller hospital, which meant I wouldn't get shoved to one department and stuck there for a couple of years. I got to help so many different kinds of people with all types of problems.

And, when I finished my residency and officially became Jordan Junco, MD, I would be making enough money to donate toward people who needed help with their medical bills, just like Mom and I had needed the help once upon a time.

I left the room so a nurse could discharge Mr. Fredericks from the ER and walked toward the bathroom. But instead of hiding in one of the stalls, I walked into a rarely used closet that held extra crutches. Some of these had to be at least fifty years old, made of wood with old rags taped over the top.

I glanced at my phone. 7:20. I was late, as usual. A missed call was right under the time, along with a text from Kai.

Kai: Can you be back by 9? I have a surprise for you. :)

I frowned at his message. There was no way I'd be getting back by nine. The drive home alone took me forty-five minutes, and I still had some paperwork to file once this call was over.

Jordan: I'm going to be later than that. Lots of paperwork. Don't wait up.

I tapped into the group call and saw my friends' faces appear on the screen. It had been way too long since we'd all spoken on the phone, much less in person. They came to the hospital on Christmas to have dinner with me since I had a shift to do, and that had only lasted an hour, including the tearful goodbye.

"Hey!" I said, waving.

They smiled at me, offering greetings of their own. I took in the backgrounds of their calls. Zara must have been in an office, bookshelves lining the walls and a pencil stuck behind her ear. Callie seemed to be at a table with a painting hanging in the corner of the screen. Rory was in her room at home leaned back against a plush headboard, and Ginger was outside on their porch swing. I'd only been to their new house a couple times, but it was idyllic there.

"Fill me in!" I said. "What did I miss?"

Zara spoke up. "I'm trying to snag a deal with a major name. Rory is painting a mural for her nephew, Ginger's wrapping up filming an ad for a major blue-jean brand, and Callie's quitting her job."

My mouth fell open. "You're quitting? I thought you were loving it."

Callie's eyes turned down. "I haven't wanted to admit how hard it is for me."

I nodded, totally understanding. Working in a service position was challenging. You give so much of yourself, and at the end of the day, some people were better off trying something new before they depleted themselves. "I've had a few people from my class already saying they're getting out of patient care as soon as they graduate. They're going to try and get in research labs."

Callie nodded. "So I'm not the only failure." She tried to smile, but the pain was clear in her voice.

Rory said, "You're not a failure. Your heart is so big. Some things I saw when I was student teaching at inner-city schools in LA..." She shook her head. "I think I'd quit too if I hadn't gotten the job I did."

Wiping at her eyes with a napkin, Callie said, "That makes me feel better."

A text notification slid over my phone from Kai.

Kai: Don't worry. I won't.

I must have made a face because Zara said, "What's going on, Jordan?"

I let out a sigh. "This clinical rotation has been

intense. Long hours at the hospital, away from Kai, and two hours of commuting every day."

Ginger gave me a wry smile. "But you love it."

I grinned back. "I love it. And things have been hard with Kai, but this is just for a little while. We've already been together for six and a half years. We'll get through this too." *And if we couldn't, we'd both be okay*, I thought to myself.

"How's your mom?" Rory asked. "I saw her at the grocery store with her new man. He is *cute*. You know, for a forty-something guy."

Now I rolled my eyes outright. "They're like teenagers. She's always giggling and sitting in his lap and taking selfies to share on 'the gram.'"

"Aw," Zara said, "I think that's cute. She deserves a love story after everything you both went through."

I shook my head. "Cute is a new puppy. Cute is a little bob haircut. This is just over the top. And his proposal—"

"They're engaged?!" Callie cried. "How did I not know this?"

"I'm not sure," I replied, "because he asked her with skywriting while they were sailing on a yacht by Brentwood Marina. Three local stations covered it."

The girls let out happy sighs for my mom. And I was happy for her too, but sometimes I missed the days when it was just her and me and our little one-bedroom apartment. Things were hard then, but simpler. I didn't have to share her with Javier and his bratty teenage daughter.

A new call came through my screen, and I drew my eyebrows together. "Hey, Birdie's calling me."

"Me too," Rory said.

"Same here," Ginger added. "Let's answer it. It'll be like old times."

I smiled, thinking back to the beginning days of the Curvy Girl Club when our high school guidance counselor, Birdie Bardot, always had our backs. I swiped to answer, and we entered a new video call with Birdie. She looked just as young as ever, with her bright blond curls and a pink bandana wrapped around her head.

But the closer I looked, the more I noticed the worry in her eyes. "What's going on, Birdie?"

"Waldo's Diner burned down."

FOUR
GINGER

I COVERED my mouth with my hand at the news. "Ray's a volunteer firefighter. Do they need help? Is the fire still going? I can have him drive into town!"

Birdie sadly shook her head. "EPD is working on it now, but it looks like a total loss."

Rory asked, "Is everyone okay?"

She nodded. "Everyone got out with no injuries. Even Grandpa Chester. We're so lucky he didn't fall or get caught up with his walker."

"What happened?" Jordan asked.

"There was an electrical issue behind the range, and it was too far gone by the time they realized what was happening."

I shook my head, picturing Waldo's Diner, where the five of us had spent so much time after football games drinking milkshakes and gabbing about life. Flashes of black and white checkered floors covered in ashen debris filled my mind, followed by pleather booths singed to crackly oblivion and then the sweet old man who made a place that felt like home leaning against his walker, watching it all engulfed by flames.

"I'm so sorry," I said. "It's completely awful. Is there anything we can do?"

Birdie shook her head again. "Right now, we're speaking with insurance about the contents. He rented the building, so the owners are handling that part. I just wanted you girls to know before you saw it on social media or the news. I know how special that place was to all of you."

"Thank you," Zara said. "And please, let us know if we can help in any way."

"Absolutely," she replied and ended the call. The five of us got back on a group call, but the line was completely silent, like there were no words to process what had happened.

Waldo's Diner had been a getaway for us. A place we could always meet for friendship and good food. A place we could count on seeing Chester's smiling face as we walked through the doors.

Rory said, "I hope Chester and Karen are going

to be okay. I don't know if the restaurant was their sole income or not..."

Jordan looked thoughtful. "Hopefully, they have some social security income."

Callie frowned. "That's hardly ever enough to live on."

"I just keep thinking there has to be something we can do," I said.

Zara nodded. "Let's come up with something. Maybe we can grab lunch at the Heywood hospital again to chat it over? We can always video call you in, Cal."

"Great," she said.

I glanced over my shoulder toward the front door. It was already dark outside, and I needed to tell Ray the news before he went to sleep. He always went to bed early since his days often started before dawn.

"I've got to go," I said. "Jordan, why don't you text us with a few times you're free since your schedule seems to be the least flexible."

Jordan nodded against a backdrop of medical supplies. "I will."

"Bye," I said, lifting my fingers to wave. "Talk soon."

I pressed the side button on my phone and got

up off the porch swing to go inside. As I walked through our bright yellow front door, I couldn't help but empathize with Chester. It would feel awful if the brand-new home Ray and I had built on his family's property got destroyed. Some things were worth so much more than money.

I walked through our kitchen with tan tile floors to hide the dirt that inevitably came in when you lived on a farm, shutting an open oak cabinet door as I passed. (Ray may have been perfect for me, but he still left doors and drawers open like it was his job.) I went to the living room to check the couch in case he was watching TV but found the room empty.

I smiled at the picture frames that already hung in the hallway leading to our four bedrooms, hopefully to be filled with children someday. Our wedding photos were my favorite. We'd exchanged vows on the Sadler Farm, and even though Ray's dad couldn't be there, I felt his spirit in the soft breeze that tickled the grass. The birds that chirped in the trees. The smile on my handsome fiancé-turned-husband's face.

The biggest photo was of us in front of a rustic alter Ray and his brother Colton made by hand. Ray had been so thoughtful that day, giving me a custom leather purse I still used today with a heart-felt note tucked inside. I had framed the letter, and it still sat on my nightstand to remind me of all his love for me.

When I walked into the bedroom, Ray was already under the covers, a booklight and book propped on his lifted knees.

"Hey," I said, walking in.

He set the book on his stomach, pages down, and turned a breathtaking smile on me. "Hey, beautiful. Thought you'd be up gabbing all night."

I shook my head, lifting the covers and climbing in beside him. He set his book on the nightstand and took me in his arms, holding me close.

"How are the girls?" he asked.

"They're good, but Birdie called us while we were talking and told us Waldo's Diner burned down."

A line formed between his eyebrows. "That's horrible. Everyone okay?"

I nodded, snuggling deeper into his arms. "But the restaurant's gone. It's a total loss."

He ran his hand over my hair, holding me tight. "That's awful. Anything we can do?"

"She said no, but I can't help thinking there has

to be something. Even just a fundraiser to help Chester and Karen."

"That's a good point. We could do a spaghetti dinner like Mom just had for the Mavens. I think that raised two thousand dollars. It's not a restaurant, but it's not nothing either."

I looked up into Ray's deep blue eyes. I loved this man with all I had. Not just because of how he cared for me, but because of how willing he was to care for everyone around him. "I love that idea... I still can't believe it happened."

"Should we go check it out?" he asked.

I glanced at the clock, seeing it was nearly nine. "It's so late. You have an early day."

"I have a wife I love," he replied, already standing up and slipping into his sandals he wore around the house. "Let's go. Maybe we'll think of something to do on the way."

My eyes filled with tears as I looked at him. He was strong and had plenty of muscles to evidence all the long hours of work he put in on the ranch, but the best parts of him were all under the surface. "I love you, Ray."

He came to me and kissed me deeply. "I love you too. Now get in the truck."

I smiled, getting my shoes on too, and following

him outside. The only lights were his mom's house a few hundred yards away. Colton lived with her while he was saving to have his own house built, and Jonah was only ten. Laura was gone, working at an equine center in Kansas. We still saw her at holidays and visited when we could get someone to cover the ranch.

Ray opened the truck door for me, and I got in, reaching across the center console to twist the keys. Headlights flooded the yard, along with the sounds of the engine, and Ray jumped in, driving down the dirt road and putting on his seatbelt as he went.

I didn't want to be apart from him, so I flipped up the center console and sat in the middle seat, the buckle around my waist and his arm around my shoulders.

"You know," I said, "the girls and I used to drink milkshakes at Waldo's and talk about you, before you and I were together."

He raised an eyebrow, glancing away from the road to give me a quizzical look. "Is that so?"

"Yep." I nodded. "I remember back when you started walking me into school."

"Because that asshole kept bothering you. Not that he's still an asshole, but then he fit the bill."

"Right. I didn't understand why you were doing it, and they said I should just ask you."

He scratched my shoulder with his fingers. "You didn't need to. It was plain as day that I was falling for you and just wanted an excuse to spend more time with you."

I smiled. He had just been some grumpy cowboy back then. Now, he was my best friend. "I like spending time with you now more than I did then."

"Hey," he said, chuckling. "At least I grew out of my attitude."

"Sure you did," I teased.

We reached the Heywood city limits, passing by the hospital where Jordan was working. Her car was out front in the parking lot, still a simple sedan despite the fact that her mom was making enough to afford so much more and she herself was dating a literal billionaire. Although, he may not have been anymore for all the charitable donations he'd been making. Last I knew, they were naming an entire hospital in LA after the Rushes. That couldn't have been cheap.

"Do you think Kai could just pay to take care of it?" Ray asked, following my gaze.

"Jordan would never let that happen."

"Why?" he asked. "That girl is so weird about money."

I kind of agreed. "It's a pride thing to her. She wants to do things on her own, and if Kai throws money at it, she feels like she hasn't earned it."

"But it's not about her. It's about Chester and Karen."

"Good point," I said, tucking it into my back pocket for a list of ideas.

We drew closer and closer to Waldo's Diner, and my chest got tight, keeping me from talking. Ray moved his arm to hold my hand and laced his fingers through mine. I knew I'd be okay, no matter what, with him at my side. But Chester and Karen, I wasn't so sure...

Then I saw it, the smoldering rubble of the diner. Smoke was still lifting from the metal hull left of the building.

I covered my mouth with my free hand, tears already springing to my eyes. "Oh my gosh, Ray... Oh my gosh."

He parked his pickup in the next building's parking lot and got out. There were a few people looking at the restaurant, and I searched for Chester and Karen but didn't see them. Thank goodness. I didn't think I could bare seeing the despair in their eyes that I felt so sharply in my heart.

But when we got closer, there was someone I recognized. Rory, dressed in sweats, standing alone and staring at the burning building with tear streaks on her cheeks.

"Rory," I said, going to her and hugging her tight. We held on for a few moments, and Rory stepped back, wiping at her eyes.

"I just had to see it for myself."

"Me too," I said, standing with an arm around her and holding on to Ray's hand for dear life.

"Everything's different," she said.

I nodded. A few minutes was all it took for everything to change.

I SAT in bed cocooned in light pink silken sheets with a horror show playing on the TV. The only problem was that this scene was unfolding on a news station, because it was happening in real life.

The camera panned over the smoldering ashes, smoke rising from what had once been one of my favorite places in the world. Tears rolled down my cheeks as I thought of Chester sitting by himself in a booth one moment and the next, seeing his life's work go down in flames.

I heard the front door opening, and I lifted the remote to turn off the TV. "Ronan?"

"It's me," he called.

I waited in silence as he slipped off his shoes, went to the sink for a glass of water and downed it as he did every evening when he got home. Then he walked to our room, slipped out of his clothes, and slid under the sheets next to me in his underwear.

He drew me close to him and kissed me slowly, his hand winding around my neck, his warm body pressing to mine.

We cuddled, kissed every night, no matter how late we got home. It was everything to Ronan to know we had a loving household, exactly the opposite of how he grew up.

He pulled back mere inches from me and said, "How was your day?" My lips quivered, instantly giving me away, and his face fell. "What's wrong?" he asked.

"Waldo's Diner... it burned down."

Memories flipped through his dark eyes as clearly as if they were made of mirrors. Us together at the restaurant, eating breakfast after our first time. The news announcing my engagement to Ryde Alexander. Ronan walking away.

Chester, sweet Chester, driving me to safety.

There were hard memories there, but good ones too. And that was life. The good and the bad, beautiful and ugly all mixed together with checkered tile floors and boomerang-stamped laminate tabletops.

"Is everyone okay?" he asked, almost holding his breath as he waited for my answer.

I nodded, turning the TV back on. "I've been watching footage on the news, and it's breaking my heart."

"Of course it is." He pulled me to his chest, hugging me tight. The old Zara would have been strong, put on a brave face. But Ronan had shown me it was safe to be real with my feelings. So instead, I broke down and cried.

I'm not sure how long we stayed like that, holding each other and watching the news, but eventually, I fell asleep dreaming of fires and friends and wishing there was something I could do.

And then I woke up to Ronan bringing me a steaming chai latte.

I rubbed my eyes, sitting up in bed. As I took the mug from him, I realized he was already dressed for the day in dark jeans and a T-shirt. The writer's room was pretty informal, not like the production room where I had to dress my best every day.

"Thank you," I said and took a sip. It was delicious, as always. He drank from his own travel mug —black coffee like the moody writer he was. I loved teasing him about that. But today... today I was sad. "I wish I didn't have to go into work. I feel like I should be doing something. Helping somehow, you know?"

"I'm sure there will be an opportunity." He took a sip from his coffee and walked to the window that overlooked downtown LA. "Why don't you see if you can meet with the girls for supper again?"

"That's a good idea... but only if you see me for dessert." I winked.

He purred.

And I laughed so hard I nearly spilled my drink.

I had to leave straight from work to meet my friends at La Belle, and driving through LA during rush hour was not the best. I wished I could be on the back of Ronan's motorcycle, zipping easily through traffic.

He'd been so busy in the writing room for this new book adaptation series that we'd hardly had time for rides along the coast. It was amazing, though, seeing him lead the room after spending a year as an intern four years as a contributing writer and now being a senior writer.

We kept things professional at work and then came home together, partners in every sense of the word. The only thing that was missing, as my dad liked to remind me, was a ring. But I didn't need to get married as long as I was living the kind of life I wanted to live.

Ronan had given me that, and so much more.

I finally reached La Belle and pulled up alongside the curb. A cute valet driver took my keys and gave me a card to pick up my car later.

I looked around the entrance as I walked in—it had been far too long since I'd spent any real amount of time in Emerson. I missed it. Things were so much simpler then, getting to spend time with my friends, hanging out in the hot tub at my house, cooking up schemes to help the girls find love.

The hostess greeted me and said, "Do you have a reservation?"

I nodded. "Under Bhatta."

She gave me an amicable smile. "Three in your party have already arrived."

Of course I was late. That much was the same.

We reached a booth in the corner, and my friends stood up, hugging me tight. Just like me, Jordan was dressed for work, but instead of dress clothes, she had on light blue scrubs covered by a black jacket. Rory looked cute in a flowy skirt and a silk blouse, and Ginger wore a button shirt with the sleeves rolled and blue jeans with boots.

"Howdy, partner," I teased.

She rolled her eyes. "I look like a country bumpkin next to the big city girl!"

I laughed, sliding into the booth next to her. Rory and Jordan sat across from us, and it felt great being all together. Almost. The only person missing was...

"Mind if I join?" Callie asked.

I turned to see her standing next to our table and squealed. "Callie! I didn't know you were coming!"

She grinned. "I thought I would surprise everyone."

Ginger and I slid down the long booth, making room for her. As she sat down next to me, I put my arm around her, squeezing her tight. "The only way it could get more perfect was if we could be sitting at Waldo's."

Jordan nodded. "I miss it already. Have there been any talks of what's going to happen next?"

With a frown, Rory said, "I talked to Birdie today at school, and she said that the insurance money will only cover what was inside the restaurant, and there's already someone offering to buy the property from the landlord. I guess they want to make it into some kind of drive-through chain."

"What?" Ginger said. "The place is still smoking and some vulture's already trying to swoop in and take it over?"

Rory nodded sadly.

"Wait, I'm confused," I said. "Didn't Chester own the restaurant?"

"He did," Rory said, "but he rented the building from the owners. The original Waldo's grandchildren. And whoever's trying to buy it is offering fifty thousand over what the property is assessed for. It'll be a pretty penny for them—insurance money and a big sale."

Callie shook her head. "All the while, Chester is without a job or business to take care of him and Karen."

It made me sick. "We have to do something about it." I looked at Jordan. "Can't you and Kai just buy the property and be Chester's new landlord?" Out of all of us, they easily had the most money to handle it.

Jordan frowned. "Kai invested almost all his money into this new app he's creating. It's supposed to have a big payoff, but that won't be for another year, at least."

Rory said, "Birdie told me her parents couldn't afford to buy the property either. I guess their company took a pretty big hit during the pandemic."

"We can't afford it either. The studio just invested in a book from a big-name author."

Ginger said, "All our money's wrapped up in the farm."

Callie added, "Invisible Mountains isn't set up to support this kind of project."

A server came by, breaking up our conversation long enough to take our drink orders, and then walked away. We sat in bleak silence for a moment. Could Waldo's Diner really be gone for good?

No.

It couldn't.

I'd practically grown up in that restaurant, had some of my best and worst memories there, and other teens deserved to have that experience too. Chester deserved to have his livelihood, and his employees deserved to have a *good* place to work.

"Then it's up to us," I said. "We'll raise the money to save Waldo's Diner."

"HOW COULD we raise half a million dollars?" I said. That number seemed imaginary, especially since we didn't have long to raise so much.

Jordan added, "Half a million just to buy the lot. That's not even counting the cost it will take to rebuild the diner and replace everything in it."

Zara shrugged like six figures was no big deal. "We live in one of the richest areas in California. It would take one person with a big heart and deep pockets to fully fund the project."

Callie set her drink down and said, "She does have a point. My dad has always talked about how much easier it is to raise money when there's a good cause involved. Chester is a great guy, and he's given so much to the community without most people ever knowing that he's the one behind it."

I could already see the wheels turning in Ginger's head as she said, "We could make some really great video content for this. Talking about Chester and Karen and how much they've dedicated to the community. We could even get kids to come on and talk about how much fun they've had visiting the diner with their parents, having milkshakes after games and things like that. Maybe even some local business owners who, like, got the idea for their businesses or worked in Waldo's with the free Wi-Fi. The employees could share what an amazing working environment it's been, since there's practically no turnover... And I haven't told anyone this, but Chester's been paying to have catered meals in the A/V room for all the Curvy Girl Clubs after us."

My jaw dropped open. I knew Birdie had been bringing marginalized girls together, but I had no idea Chester was the one funding it. "Are you serious?"

Ginger nodded. "Cori told me about it. Chester wanted to keep it on the down-low, but after hearing from Birdie how much of a difference it made for each of us, Chester said he wanted to help."

Zara leaned in closer, meeting each of our eyes. "Chester has changed lives with Waldo's Diner. That can't be over now, right?"

Jordan frowned. "I'm not sure how much time we have to dedicate to something like this. I'm really busy with med school, and my relationship's hanging on by a thread because of it."

My heart ached for her. "You and Kai are having troubles?"

She kept her eyes on her hands as she nodded. "I can't blame him for being distant. We hardly ever see each other, and it's hard to come in second to my work all the time."

Zara chewed on her lip. "What if it didn't have to take that long? Rory has spring break in a couple weeks, don't you?" I nodded. "And Callie, how long are you here?"

"As long as I need," she answered.

"Well then, let's see if we can get it done by the end of spring break," Zara said.

I raised my eyebrows. "You want us to raise half a million dollars, and then some, in *less than a month*?" This girl had to be crazy.

She had a wicked grin on her face. "Why the hell not?"

Callie said, "I'm in. I don't have anything better to do, and it would be really good to work on something where I can tell if I've succeeded."

Ginger looked between the two of them. "I'm wrapping up the jeans commercial at the end of this week, and then I'm all yours."

I shook my head, amazed by their determination. "I'll help however I can."

We were all quiet as we waited for Jordan to pitch in. But she slowly shook her head. "I have my mom's engagement party and I was supposed to spend the rest this weekend with Kai. I'm worried that he'll be upset if we don't get to spend time together."

"Then bring him along," Zara said. "I'm sure we could use his computer savvy to help set up a website or maybe even social media accounts and things like that. And maybe working together on something will help remind him that you're both on the same team."

Jordan nodded, a small smile on her face. "That's a good idea. If I can get him on board, I'm in."

"Great," Zara said. "What else? What are we missing?"

Callie said, "Should we talk to Chester? Make sure that he is okay with us doing all of this?"

Zara nodded, pulling out her phone to take notes. "Can you handle that?"

Callie said, "Sure. It'll probably be good for me to go and visit him anyway. I wonder how he's holding up."

I frowned. "According to Birdie, he's just in shock. I can't imagine everything changing so quickly."

But then again, I could. That was what infertility was like. One minute, you're planning your entire life. Thinking about all the kids you'll have, how they'll have their father's eyes and your smile and how you'll go on family vacations together and what a great uncle your brother will be. And the next second... it's all ripped away with a negative test.

I didn't want to do IVF. I didn't want to take any more medications. I just wanted my child. My family.

Food arrived at the table, and we ate together, agreeing to meet over the weekend to come up with a gameplan. As soon as we paid, I needed to go home. Beckett was supposed to be getting in this evening, and I was still in my fertile window. I hoped tonight would be the night. The miracle night that started our family.

So I told the girls goodbye, got into my car, and drove back to our house. I grinned at the sight of Beckett's car parked outside. I turned off my engine and ran through the door to give him a hug. So much had happened, and I just needed to feel his support, his love.

He grinned, picking me up and spinning me around. "I missed you way too much."

"I missed you too," I replied, burying my nose into his chest and breathing in his smell. Our smell.

That was one of the funny things about getting older with someone. I used to be so intoxicated by his cologne, by the sight of him. Now, we used the same laundry detergent. His cologne sat on the bathroom counter for me to smell any time I liked. Now that been together so long, I still loved the little things like the way his hair looked fresh out of the shower or how good he looked in gray sweatpants, but his presence was the best part of being married. It comforted me in a way that nothing else could. He was mine as much as I was his.

He bent down and kissed me, and I tilted my

chin up to kiss him back. I loved this stance. The feeling of our bodies pressed together and the tangle of our tongues. The way he held me so carefully and so passionately at the same time.

I pulled back from his kiss and said, "My temperature chart said I'm ovulating." I grinned, taking his hand. "Want to take this to the bedroom?"

He frowned, standing utterly still.

Wondering what had changed in the last two seconds, my eyebrows drew together. "What's wrong?"

He let out a sigh. "Sit with me?" he asked, taking my hand and pulling me toward our kitchen table.

I followed him, despite the doubt in my mind screaming at me to stop. Like if we just stood here in our front entrance, he wouldn't be able to tell me whatever bad news I could feel was coming.

We sat in the chairs I'd hand painted, and again, I asked, "What's going on?" I could feel my fertile window slipping away with every beat of my dread-filled heart.

He held my hand in both of his, looking down at our joined fingers, and then he finally met my eyes. "Rory, I think I need a break."

His words were like a punch to the gut, no matter how gently they'd been delivered. "A break from me?" Tears burned in my eyes.

"No, no, no," he said quickly, bringing my hands to his mouth and kissing them. "I just want to be *us* again. It never used to feel like anything was missing. It felt like love, just you and me against the world. And now, with all this trying for a baby, it just makes me more and more aware of all the ways you think we aren't enough."

I could hardly breathe, could hardly speak. Losing him would be a nightmare worse than death... but never having a family? My voice cracked as I said, "I thought you wanted a child too."

He tilted his head, looking me in the eyes. "I wanted you to be happy." He tried to cup the back of my neck with this hand, but I shied away. Looking hurt, he dropped his hand to his side and said, "I love you, but I can't see you cry every month. I can't make love with you knowing that you're not there for the moment but for the result. I need some time to feel like you love just me again."

I shook my head quickly, not wanting to hear any of the words he had to say, not wanting to feel the hurt he was sending my way. "I love you, Becks.

I never wanted you to feel like you weren't good enough."

"Then why can't we just let it happen when it happens? Why does there have to be all the tracking and the medication and the scheduled sex?"

"I love you so much, and I want to experience parenthood with you. Is that so wrong?"

He held both my hands again, and this time, I didn't pull away. "If you love me, then love me. Not what I can give you or can't."

I hated when he acted this way, like it was his fault we weren't getting pregnant. I was the faulty one. The broken one. "You know it's me. I'm the one with PCOS. We've known that forever."

"You've been ovulating, and I've never been tested," he said. "And besides, it doesn't matter. You want something that, clearly, I can't give you."

"What can I do to convince you?" I asked. "What would be good enough to show you that I can handle this? I won't cry every time I get my period. I'll get a therapist, a mindset coach, whatever you need."

"If you want to show me something, show me that you can have a life outside of a baby. Because the truth is, it might never happen for us, and I want to know that we'll be enough. Forever."

I stared at his hands on mine, the hands I had held for years now. The hands that had touched me so gently, so kindly, so lovingly. And even though those hands had never hurt me, his words were tearing me apart.

I felt it too, the fatigue of trying and failing month after month. I had just thought that it was worth it if we eventually got the family we wanted. But for him to keep trying to give me that family, he wanted me to focus on something else. So I would.

I looked up at him and said, "The girls and I are going to raise money to save Waldo's Diner."

He kissed my forehead and gave me a genuine smile. "See? That's exactly what I was talking about. This is going to be so good for you, babe."

I smiled as best I could and nodded. "You've had a long trip, honey. Why don't you go shower and I'll meet you in bed for a movie or something?"

"Sounds great." He left to our bathroom, and I waited until the shower had turned on to cry. I felt alone in the kitchen, and I wondered if I would feel this alone for the rest of my life.

SEVEN
CALLIE

I BLINKED MY EYES OPEN, staring up at the ceiling of my childhood bedroom. The One Direction posters were gone, but I could still see the little pin holes from the thumbtacks that had kept them up.

Other things about the room had changed. All my clothes were gone, and the drawers had been filled with materials for Mom's embroidery projects (her new obsession post-sugar cookie decorating). The photos had been taken down and moved with me to North Carolina. Now Mom had hung pictures from my wedding, Joe and Gemma's elopement, and their first two grandchildren.

I couldn't wait to see them over the weekend. They lived in LA now, just an hour's drive away, which my mother loved, especially now that grand-babies were involved.

They all seemed so happy that I had held back my news, trying not to bring them down with my sadness. My failure.

But I could see the questions in my mom's eyes last night when she picked me up from the airport. I'd avoided them only by saying I didn't want to talk about it and be sad before dinner with the girls, but I knew she was downstairs, waiting for me. I could tell by the scent of bacon and pancakes in the air.

With a sigh, I rolled out of bed and went to my open suitcase, pulling out a pair of shorts and a T-shirt. I took them with me to the bathroom, showering and getting ready for the day. Everything about me felt tired, like I was coming back to life after years of hibernation. Of being worn down until there was nothing left of me.

But it felt good too, like I was in a place where I could rebuild my life, with Carson by my side.

With a towel in my hair, I walked back to my room to apply my psoriasis lotion and dialed his number. When he answered, I could hear the sounds of the gym in the background, but most of all, I could hear the love in his voice.

"Hey, baby," he said.

I smiled, instantly lightened. "I miss you."

"I miss you too. This is the longest we've been apart since Joe and Gemma had Nichole."

"I know." I sat on the edge of the bed, thinking of how nice it had been to be away from my job for a week last year, while I helped with my new niece. "It's nice being back here, even though it's different."

"Yeah?"

"It just feels like home," I said quietly. It almost felt bad to admit that North Carolina never really felt like home in the same way Emerson did.

"That's good. Maybe being somewhere more comfortable will help you recover and get some perspective on what you want to do next."

"I hope so," I said. Because right now, I was lost in more ways than I cared to admit.

There was some noise in the background of the call, and Carson said, "Sorry, I need to get back to it. I love you. Text me anytime, okay?"

"I will," I promised, and we hung up. Taking a deep breath, I stood and let my hair out of my towel before going downstairs.

Mom was sitting at the table, looking at her phone with a coffee mug in one hand. At the sound of my footsteps, she looked up at me, smiling. "I'm so glad you're awake. I was starting to worry I made breakfast too soon."

"You're going to spoil me," I replied. The only time Carson and I ever made good breakfasts like this was on the weekends after sleeping in.

"Good, maybe then I can convince you to stay." She winked and got up, going to the kitchen. "How many pancakes do you want?"

"Two," I said. "And lots of coffee. Do you still have that big soup mug?"

She laughed. "Giant bowl of coffee coming up."

I sat at the table, looking around to see what else had changed in my childhood home. There was a new painting above the table. Little felt pads under the chair legs to slide easier on the tile.

Mom came back with my plate and set it in front of me. She even took a few bites of her own breakfast before starting the questioning.

"I have to ask, honey. What's going on with your job? Is everything okay with Carson?"

I finished chewing my pancake and took a sip of coffee, bracing myself for the truth. For her reaction. "Mom, I quit my job." Concern laced her expression, but I quickly continued. "It's been eating me alive. I wanted to help kids like Carson, but the further I get into it, the less I think that's what I'm doing. I'm not sure what I want to do for work yet, but I know this isn't it. And I know that you and Dad invested so much into my education, but—"

"Honey, honey," Mom said gently. She reached across the table for my hand, and I placed it in hers, tears already stinging my eyes. "You can't put yourself through misery because a few years ago, Dad and I helped you with college."

My jaw shook. "I don't want you to have *wasted* so much money on me."

"That money could never be wasted, Callie. You learned so much while you were getting your degree. How to live on your own, how to navigate a classroom with hundreds of students, how to start something and see it through to the end. And then, in the last couple years of work, you've navigated so many stressors, life as a newlywed, moving across the country, budgeting your new lifestyle your husband. We're amazed by you and completely in support of whatever direction you choose to go from here. Life is an education all its own. Sometimes the biggest lesson you can learn is the importance of choosing to do what makes you happy."

Tears streamed down my cheeks as I got up

from my seat to go give her a hug. She'd been so gracious with me. Exactly the kind of mom I hoped to be someday. "I love you so much."

"I love you too," she said, rubbing my back and holding me close. When I stepped back and went to my chair, she smiled. "This is exciting, Callie."

I gave a halfhearted laugh, wiping at my eyes with a napkin. "Exciting? Learning that I'm starting from scratch after six years?"

Mom grinned. "Exactly. That means anything is possible from here."

Mom and I spent most of the morning talking, just catching up on what life was like for her and Dad in Emerson and what Carson and I were up to in North Carolina. I had to cut it short so I could go visit Chester and Karen.

They were making tea and biscuits for me—how could they be so giving after such a big setback—and I didn't want to be late.

They lived in an older part of Emerson, where the trees were tall and thick and the streets wound with less organization than the new housing developments had. My phone took me to a house on the corner, and I smiled at their home.

It was a cute white bungalow with blue shutters and colorful flowers growing all about the front. A bright blue table and chairs sat on the front porch, and I pictured Chester and Karen drinking their morning coffee there. The entire place looked like happily ever after.

I got out of my car and walked to the front door, feeling a strange mix of light and heavy. I was excited to see them after being away for so long, but the devastation they must have felt at losing their livelihood...

I took a deep breath and pressed the doorbell. Within seconds, Karen was at the door. I'd only seen her in person a couple times before, but she was a beauty with her long white hair tied in a bun and a contagious smile that touched every corner of her face.

"Hi, Callie, come on in," she said.

"Hi there," I said, stepping through the door onto hardwood floors. "Thank you so much for having me."

"Oh, honey, we're happy to have you. I think Chester's missed being around people at the diner." She led me through a foyer filled with framed art and photos and into a dining room that overlooked a backyard full of greenery.

Chester pressed himself up from the table and extended his arms for a hug. I squeezed him, realizing how much older he'd gotten. He was shorter now than he'd been even a year ago. Thinner too.

"It's so good to see you, honey," Chester said.

"I'm glad you're okay. I'm so sorry about what happened."

He looked sad as he sat back at the table. "I keep thinking it over, wondering how I could have stopped it from happening, but the insurance company said it was a faulty electrical line behind the stove. Nothing anyone could have done."

I sat across from him while Karen moved to the kitchen, getting a teapot from the stove.

"Callie, do you prefer a black tea, green tea, maybe Earl Grey?"

"Earl Grey is great," I said. "Thank you."

She began pouring cups, and Chester said, "Tell me about you, sweetheart. How are you and Carson doing on the East Coast?"

"Missing home mainly," I admitted. "I'm not so sure I was cut out to be a social worker, so now I'm taking a break, trying to figure it all out."

He nodded. "Sometimes it takes trying a lot of different things before you find the one that sticks."

"Is that how it worked for you?" I asked.

He nodded. "I started my first job at twelve, helping my dad at the lumberyard. Running and fetching things mostly. Then I worked at a construction site. Then one of my coworkers started a business sourcing materials for eco-friendly builds. It was really new back then, groundbreaking. So then I was on as a consultant for those types of projects until I retired."

Karen brought us both cups and put her hands on his shoulders. "Need anything else?"

He patted her hand. "Not for me."

"Me neither," I said. "Thank you."

"Of course." Karen sat with us. "Chester couldn't stay retired for long."

He chuckled. "I started going into Waldo's every day because I was so damn bored, and then the owner, kind of joking, said, 'You're here so often, you should run the place.' And I thought, why, yeah, I could do that. Pretty soon, we were drawing up papers so I could rent the business from him, and well, here we are now. Waldo isn't alive now, but his granddaughter honored the agreement. Until now."

"Birdie said someone's looking to buy the land to put in a drive-through?"

"Someone with deep pockets thinks it's a good location for a coffee place," he said.

I shook my head. "What if someone could buy it for you? Let you run Waldo's again?"

He reached across the table, holding his wife's hand. The love between them made my heart swell. I hoped Carson and I looked at each other like that in all the years to come. "I'd say it would be a miracle, but I think I've already gotten plenty of those in my lifetime."

I smiled between the two of them. "Well, the girls and I are planning a miracle."

EIGHT

JORDAN

I GRABBED my bag and went to the staff bathroom at Heywood Hospital to change for my mother's engagement party. They'd scheduled it for a Saturday night so I could make it, but honestly, I wished they wouldn't have.

All of Javier's giant family would be there, and I knew I would feel like an outsider with only Kai by my side.

As I shimmied out of my light blue scrub pants, my phone chimed, and I lifted it to see a new message in the group chat.

Callie: I went and talked to Chester and Karen today. They said they're honored that we care so much about helping them out. It's a go on their end!

I wanted to be happy about it, I did, but all I felt

was the pressure of more work on my shoulders. And it wasn't that I minded work, but I'd been working my whole life. First for my mom's cleaning company, then for good grades in college so I could get into med school, then studying rigorously so I could do well in med school and make the most of my clinical rotations.

I wanted being a doctor to be my only job, so I'd have more time for friends, family, vacations, romance. I just hoped Kai would hang on long enough for us to do that together.

Another text went off, and I looked at my phone.

Zara: Great. Let's meet at my apartment tomorrow. We can spend the day making a game plan for the fundraiser.

The other girls replied that they'd be there, and I did the same. Even though I hadn't brought it up to Kai yet. We were supposed to spend the day together, and we would be, just not the way he had planned.

I took deep breaths, trying to lower the stress that always seemed to find me, and finished putting on my black dress. Then I slipped on some wedge sling backs and undid my hair from the claw clip it had been in all day.

As I looked in the mirror, dabbing on lip gloss, I became a completely different person. Dr. Junco to just Jordan.

I threw my scrubs and jacket and clogs into my bag and then made my way out of the hospital, waving to people as I went. I tried to remember everyone's names, from the cleaning staff to the receptionists and nurses and CNAs. It mattered to me that we all felt like we were on the same team.

As soon as the double doors slid open, I got out my phone and dialed Kai's number. Within a few rings, he answered, "Just get out?"

"I'm only a few minutes behind," I said defensively.

"I'm not mad, just checking."

I let out another breath, getting into my car and shutting the door. My phone connected to the speakers, and I said, "Sorry. I'm just stressed about tonight. Mom said there are supposed to be a hundred people there, if that tells you how outnumbered we'll be."

"A hundred? I thought it was seventy-five!"

"Apparently, they had a few last-minute additions." I put my car into gear and drove out of the parking lot. "If Mom's happy, I'm happy, but I wish it wasn't so uncomfortable to be around their family."

Javier's family came from old money, the kind where he never really had to work to get anywhere in life. He had a cushy job in the family business, a massive house to enjoy, and his teenage daughter had all the opportunities in the world but appreciated none of them.

My therapist—which was basically all the self-care I had time for these days—said it was triggering to me because of the way I grew up. Because of all the things I missed out on as a kid. I was trying not to hold that against Javier and his daughter, no matter how hard it was.

Besides, Mom had her own money now. She was a self-made woman, just like she'd always wanted to be. I was proud of her. Happy for her getting her happily ever after, even if it felt like mine was slipping out of reach.

On the other side of the phone, I could hear keys jangling. "Are you leaving the house?"

"Yeah, I should get there about the same time as you," Kai said.

"Let's talk as we drive?" I asked, hopeful. "I've missed you so much lately."

I could hear the smile in his voice as he said, "I'd like that."

"Tell me about the app. How's the coding going? Is Cody still being a jerk?"

Kai snorted. "First of all, who goes into coding if their name is Cody?"

I laughed. "His parents were probably clairvoyant."

"Either way. He came to my office today and apologized for being rude to the interns. He said his kid's been sick and his wife caught it too, so it was kind of a hellscape at his house."

"Ah," I replied. "Isn't it crazy that people our age are old enough to have kids and be married and all of that? I feel like I barely have time to take care of myself."

"I think they just make it work, prioritize the things that matter to them," Kai said, his blinker going in the background.

"True. I guess Rory and Beckett are trying for a kid, but it's not going well."

"That sucks. Maybe you could hook them up with a good fertility doctor?"

"Maybe. I think Clarissa from med school is in that field now." I stopped at a red light and glanced at the clock. I hoped traffic wouldn't be too bad in Brentwood. Mom would be so upset if I were late.

"How are the rest of the girls?" he asked.

I cringed. "Good, actually... They came up with this idea to raise money to buy Waldo's Diner out from that drive-through."

"Yeah? That's awesome. Chester and Karen are good people. They deserve that."

"In that case... Is it okay if we go to Zara's tomorrow for a strategy session?"

The line was quiet for a long moment. So long, I almost thought I lost him, but the minutes were still ticking past on my car's display.

"Kai?"

He let out a sigh. "We were supposed to spend the day together."

"I know, but we still can go together, and—"

"It's not the same. Jordan, I miss you. I want to spend time with you. I don't know why you're making it so damn hard for us to be together."

His words were like a weight to the chest. I'd never wanted to be anything but a doctor, and now he was upset about it? "It's not me! It's med school. I told you this wouldn't be easy, Kai."

"You just didn't tell me I'd be the last thing on your list."

My chest ached at his words. "Kai, you know that's not—"

"I don't want to talk right now. I'll meet you outside the restaurant."

The call ended, and I kept my eyes on the road, despite the searing pain in my heart. Despite the sinking feeling in my stomach that told me he was right. And despite the fear ripping through me that if I didn't think fast, I'd finish med school without anyone to share my life with.

The drive to View House in Brentwood felt longer than ever, but I pulled up front, and a complimentary valet took my car away. I half expected not to see Kai at all, but there he was, waiting by the door.

He wore a navy-blue suit that fit his narrow frame and made him look like... a billion dollars. When we met in high school, he wore his hair long and shaggy, but now he sported a fade on the sides of his head and longer hair on top that was carefully gelled. And his eyes, those dark almond eyes, still took my breath away as he watched me approach.

I had hoped to hug and kiss him, but he only extended his elbow for me. Wordlessly, I took it.

The entire restaurant had been booked out for

the party. It had two levels, and on the lower level, Javier's friends and family were drinking, eating appetizers off trays being carried around.

I quickly flagged down a cocktail server and took whatever alcoholic drink was on the tray. A sip told me it was a gin and tonic with a sprig of mint. Good enough for me.

Kai took one too, and we continued our path, not being greeted by anyone, not saying hello, just searching for my mom.

When we didn't see her downstairs, we went up to the higher level and quickly found her sitting at a table with Javier, his thirteen-year-old daughter, Arabella, and his mom, dressed to the hilt and decorated with strands of pearls.

"I know that you're mad, but please act like you like me," I quietly begged to Kai.

He turned to me. "I've never had to pretend."

Mom caught sight of us and stood, waving us over. "I'm so glad you two made it!" She looked so beautiful in a champagne-colored jumpsuit encrusted with sequins and jewels.

We walked to her, and she wrapped her arms around me tight, then dropped a kiss on my cheek. Her holding me so close almost tore me apart. But I needed to be strong, to be happy for the woman who raised me.

When she pulled back from me, she hugged Kai next. I noticed she was still wearing Juana's necklace that he had saved for her all those years ago.

"Sit with us," Mom said, gesturing toward the empty seats. Kai had to sit next to Arabella, leaving me next to Javier's mother.

"Did you just come from the hospital?" Mrs. Ramirez asked.

I nodded. "Just worked a full shift."

"I can tell, you poor thing. They should give you more of a break to get ready, especially for family affairs."

I bristled at the carefully veiled insult, but Kai said, "She's as beautiful as ever to me. Especially since she's making a real difference in the world."

My heart twisted at the compliment. He loved me so much. I hated that work had come between us.

"That's my baby," Mom said. "Always thinking of others."

I gave her a thankful smile. Arabella groaned. "These servers are awful. I swear my drink's been empty for five minutes now!"

Kai and I exchanged looks. This was not how

we treated people. But if it bothered my mom, she didn't let on. Mrs. Ramirez lifted her bejeweled hand in the air, scanning the room, and waved over a worker in a black suit. "Excuse me. My granddaughter's glass has been empty for quite some time now. Do I need to speak with a manager about why I spent so much money on such poor service?"

"No, ma'am," the guy said quickly. He must have been around my age, but he looked much younger under her fury. "What are you drinking, miss? I'd be happy to refill it for you."

Arabella didn't even look up from her phone. "Dr. Pepper. You really should remember these things."

"Absolutely." He took the glass away, and I stared in horrified silence. She hadn't even thanked him.

"Thank you," I called after him.

He turned just long enough to give me a grateful smile.

"Mom, how's work going?" I asked. I knew she and her best friend Camilla had been working hard on a new course on how to start your own profitable cleaning business with everything she'd learned the hard way.

Mom's eyes lit up the way they always did when

she talked about her business. "Camilla has gotten so good at customer support and managing the group. We're getting great engagement with our early members."

Javier said, "You know what I love about your mom? She could stop working right now and live a life of luxury, but she's so committed and dedicated that she's putting in just as many hours as ever."

Maybe he scored a few bonus points for that compliment.

Mom turned and kissed him, thanking him, but we both knew why she'd never stop working, never stop saving and investing. We'd been left high and dry by a man before. She'd never be caught off guard and unprepared like that again. Not if she could do something about it.

The band in the corner stopped playing, and Javier's brother spoke into the microphone. "Thank you, everyone, for coming to this engagement soiree! We're so happy for Javi to finally find someone worthwhile. And Jacinda, we're thankful you're looking the other way!" The crowd laughed, and Mom kissed Javier on the cheek.

"I remember thinking that my brother was the pickiest man on the face of the earth. He had women throwing themselves at him left and right, but he just kept saying, 'No, I'm waiting for the perfect one.' Then in walks Jacinda, speaking at Arabella's business class about being an entrepreneur, and my brother was hooked! Jaci, welcome to the family!"

Everyone cheered and toasted, but my stomach turned uncomfortably. It didn't pass my notice that he hadn't welcomed Kai and me as well. Or that he hadn't told me it was time for speeches.

I got up and walked toward the band, who had resumed playing, determined to give the speech I'd prepared for my mom, and in a lot of ways, for Kai and me as well.

The guy playing acoustic guitar was at the front, and I waved toward him. He looked up from his strings to me, still playing.

"I have a speech too," I said over the music.

He nodded and yelled at the rest of his bandmates. "Pause at the end of this song."

I stood off to the side, feeling awkward and out of place as ever, and waited for them to be done. Whey they stopped playing, he smiled and gestured toward the mic. "It's all yours."

I took a breath and stepped up onto the stage, walking to the mic stand and adjusting it so it would be the right height for me.

"Hi, everyone," I said, slowly cutting the chatter amongst the party attendants. "I don't know most of you, but I'm Jacinda's daughter, Jordan."

That caught their attention. Instead of indifference, they were looking at me like a zoo animal, studying me closely. But all I cared about was my mom and Kai several tables back. They were my people, always and forever.

"For a long time, it was just my mom and me. My little sister passed away from cancer as a child, and our father ran away, leaving us with all of our grief and a lot of medical debt." My chest felt heavy, remembering being so young and not knowing where my dad was, not quite understanding where my sister had gone. "For the next ten years of my life, Mom worked harder than I've seen anyone work. Through her grief, she loved me as more than a mom. She was my best friend. She taught me about hard work, loyalty, and commitment."

I met my mom's eyes, and she had both of her hands covering her heart.

"Relationships aren't easy. I've been with my boyfriend since we were eighteen years old. We've been through college, med school, moves, and life together. And I know if I follow my mom's guidance, I can be the woman he deserves. I can love him the way I want to.

"See, when my mom commits to something, she gives it everything she has, so I have no doubt that she will commit to this marriage, to this family, and bless everyone here in ways that you've never known.

"I want to congratulate my mom for finding someone she wants to commit to in that way, but most of all, I want to congratulate Javier and Arabella. My mom's a hell of a woman. I hope you treat her with all the love she deserves."

The crowd clapped for the speech, but my mom got up and gave me a big hug. I squeezed her back, saying into her shoulder, "I meant every word."

She held my face and kissed my forehead before letting me go. But then Kai was there, holding me tight in the middle of all Javier's family.

"I'm so sorry," I said, crying into his shoulder. "I promise you I'm here for you. I want to get this right. I'm committed to you."

Kai took a shuddering breath, speaking through his own emotion. "I love you, Jordan Junco. I always have, and I always will."

NINE

GINGER

WHILE RAY'S younger brother Colton brought water to the cattle, Ray and I drove his truck to the pasture to check the pairs. All of the heifers had calved, some within the last week, and now the mamas and babies grazed in the fields.

"I love looking at the baby calves," I said, leaning on my forearm to look out the window as he slowly drove down the trail made by years of tire treads.

Ray chuckled. "That's redundant. Calves are babies."

"You know what I mean," I said, turning back to look at him. He was so handsome with the pale morning light framing him through the window. "The *baby* babies. Their spindly legs are so stinking cute! And look at that little white patch on that one's head. *Adorable.*"

He followed my gaze to the little calf with black fur everywhere except its forehead. There was a small smile on his lips. "It is pretty cute." A line formed between his eyebrows. "Oh no."

"What?" I asked, trying to see what he was seeing.

He pointed east. "See that calf over there by itself? That's never a good sign."

My chest felt tight as he veered off the trail and drove on rough ground toward the calf. When we got about twenty yards away, he turned the pickup off and got out. I followed him, grass swishing under my boots.

The little black calf was lying in a feeble heap, letting out weak moos.

"Oh, baby," I said sadly. "What's wrong with it?"

"The mom might have rejected it, or she could be sick too. We'll have to see if we can find her."

"We can't just leave him here."

Ray shook his head. "He's coming with us." Within seconds, he'd scooped the calf up in his arms, and it barely even protested. I walked behind them toward the pickup, and Ray loaded him into the back of the truck. "I'll sit back here with him and you drive?"

I nodded, rubbing the calf's head. "You're in good hands, sweetie pie." I looked up at Ray, worried. "Do you think he'll be okay?"

Ray gave me a sad smile. "I think he has a chance."

The calf looked at me with big dark eyes, and I hoped he would make it. As I walked to the driver's seat, my eyes felt hot. That was still one part of farm life I hadn't adjusted to. Out on the farm, you had a front row seat to the circle of life—the beginning and its end. Even a couple of years out here full-time hadn't made it any easier.

I put the truck in gear and began driving through the pasture. It didn't take long to find the mom—her tag number matched his. I got out and walked back to Ray. He still had the calf in his arms. "What do we do?" I asked.

"I'll have Colton bring her to the pen by the house so we can see how she takes to him when he's feeling better."

I nodded. "I'll call the girls and tell them we can't make it today... maybe we can video in."

"Nonsense." Ray said.

I raised my eyebrows. "I'm not about to leave him here."

"Then why don't we bring him with us?"

Ray pressed his finger to the doorbell button outside of Zara's apartment.

I'd been here once before, when she first moved in a couple years ago, and it still struck me how fancy it was compared to the life I lived with Ray on the farm. She always did have a flare for the finer things in life.

She pulled the door open, looking glamorous in leggings and an oversized shirt that fell off one of her bronze shoulders. Her smile quickly fell though as her eyes landed to the right of me. "What is *that?*"

I looked at our sweet little calf, Oscar, riding in an oversized dog kennel on a luggage cart we found by the reception desk. We'd gotten so many weird looks walking into the building, but luckily, no one had stopped us. It reminded me of all those years ago in high school when Ray walked beside me so I'd be unbothered by bullies.

But the way Zara was looking at us, I couldn't

help but think this may be as far as we went. "He's sick," I said, putting out my bottom lip. "We need to give him electrolytes every three hours and lots of cuddles. His mom practically abandoned him to die!"

From behind Zara, Ronan said, "What's—" but stopped as soon as he saw us and the calf. Mirth lit up his dark eyes, and he drew his hand to his mouth.

Ray shrugged. "He can stay in the kennel, and we brought extra towels and stuff, just in case he.... you know."

Zara threw her hands up in defeat and walked away. "Come in."

We followed Ronan into their spacious living room, Ray rolling Oscar along on the cart. The other girls immediately came over, Callie putting her fingertips through the cage to scratch the top of his nose. She looked up at me, a big smile on her face. "What's his name?"

"Oscar," I said. I told them about how we found him that morning, and soon they were all cooing and scratching him.

Except Zara. She'd never been much for animals. She sat across the living room, cross-legged on her white couch, and positioned her laptop on her lap. "Okay, so I think we need to start by setting some SMART goals. Specific, Measurable, Attainable, Relevant, and Time-bound."

Jordan grinned. "Looks like those business classes are paying off."

Zara shrugged. She had started taking online classes a couple years ago and had applied all of it to her work and life.

Kai leaned back against a chair, saying, "As far as specific and measurable, you have to decide how much you want to raise and work from there."

Rory nodded and said, "Birdie connected me with the owners, and they said the buyer's offering four hundred and fifty-five thousand, so if we want a competitive offer, we need to raise at least half a million."

Zara tapped on her keyboard. "Do we have a real estate agent to draft the offer?"

"Cori just got her license," Ginger said. "I'm sure she'll waive her fee for us."

"Great." Zara typed some more.

Rory said, "And for timebound, the buyer's having an appraiser come by and inspect the lot once they get the all-clear from the insurance adjuster. We have two weeks, max, before they gave to accept the other offer."

The room fell silent aside from the silent huffs of the calf in the kennel.

"Two weeks," Beckett said. "That's going to be a lot of work."

Ronan nodded. "Are you sure you want to take this on?"

Callie said, "I don't have a job like you guys. I'm happy to take on most of the work while you're busy with your jobs."

I frowned. "Are you sure, Callie? I don't want it to be unfair for you."

"Unfair is what happened to Chester and Karen. I know it sounds crazy, but I almost feel like it was meant to be that I quit my job when I did. It's giving me a chance to do something that really matters."

Rory reached over and squeezed Callie's hand. "That's amazing of you. It'll make a real difference to them."

"I hope so," she said, reaching over to pet Oscar.

Ray stood up and said, "I need to get his electrolytes in a bottle." He walked toward the bag that he'd left near the entrance, and the rest of us kept brainstorming.

"We can do a documentary," Ginger said.

"Share it online, have a viewing at the movie theater, charge admission to get in."

Beckett nodded. "I can do photos of the burned building, maybe even some of Chester and Karen in front of it, you know, to put a real face on the devastation."

Rory rubbed his arm. "That's a great idea. I can draft an email to send to the Emerson Academy alumni directory and current students and parents. There's really not anywhere like Waldo's for the kids to hang out, and it's better than them parking at Emerson Trails."

Ray came back carrying a bottle and smirking. "As if we didn't all do that when we were in school."

Callie's cheeks were hot. "So... I can ask my dad about making the donations tax deductible. Maybe we can funnel them through Invisible Mountains and earmark them for this project."

Ronan said, "That's a good idea. And if you need help writing some copy to go with the videos and on flyers and whatnot, I can work on that. I have a friend in the marketing department who I'm sure would look them over too."

Kai said, "I can make a website to keep all the

information in one place and set up a page where everyone can see how much we have left to go."

Ray passed me the bottle, and I held it out to Oscar. He feebly took the nipple and began suckling at the liquid. Everyone was quiet for a moment as they watched, and eventually Zara said, "You'd be such a great mom, Ging."

I smiled up at her. "A child's different from a calf."

"Exactly. Imagine how much more you'd care about an actual human being."

I thanked her and turned my attention back toward Oscar. I hoped he would make it. It would gut me if he didn't.

Rory said, "Zara, what else do we need?"

"We need to start filming ASAP. Callie, can you call Chester and see if they'd be good for an interview tomorrow?"

She took out her phone, and we waited quietly while she held it to her ear. "Hey, Chester!... The girls and I got together and came up with a plan. Any chance you and Karen would be free tomorrow for some photos and an interview about the restaurant?... That would be amazing. Could we meet at your house, say nine?" She looked to Beckett and me, and we nodded, indicating that time worked. "Great! We'll see you at nine!... I hope it works too.... Bye-bye."

She hung up, and a nervous tingle went through my stomach. We were really doing this, and I'd be making a documentary—months' worth of work in days. I was so happy we finished that jeans promotion because I couldn't imagine doing both. But this was when the rubber met the road. I had people counting on me, and there was no way I'd let them down.

"Ray and I should probably get home so I can storyboard and come up with interview questions," I said.

Zara nodded. "Thanks for coming over. Can't wait to do this for the diner!"

I got up and hugged each of my friends while Ray loaded Oscar and his cage back on the bell cart. Then we walked back out of the apartment to his truck waiting in the parking lot. It looked so different than the rest of the sleek vehicles around it with its thin coat of dust and dents and scratches, but I wouldn't trade it or the man who drove it for the world.

Ray wedged Oscar's cage in the back seat, then got in the front. "Do you want to go see your parents while we're here? Emerson isn't too far out of the way."

I gave him a look. "I have way too much work to do."

"Sure that's it," he said, backing out. He clearly didn't believe me.

"Mom and I just don't see eye to eye anymore."

"As if you ever did." He put his arm up, hooking his hand on the back of my seat as he drove. "You have to forgive her eventually."

"Ray, she threw away all the cleaning supplies in our house that your mother gave to us as a house-warming gift and replaced it with *vinegar*."

"She meant well."

"She threw away my tampons!"

He chuckled. "So what if she only wants the best up there. I tend to agree."

My cheeks flushed, but the words kept tumbling out of me, demanding to be spoken. "You've heard her make those little digs about how she thinks I could do better than filming commercials on the farm. It's like nothing in my life is good enough for her or will ever satisfy her. She kept me from so much in my life, Ray. I know she thought she was protecting me, but she hurt me, and she has no intention of changing or letting me live my life the way I want to. And Dad just stands by and lets her do it."

He lowered his hand from the back of my seat to squeeze my fingers. "It doesn't matter what anyone thinks, as long as you and I are okay with the way things are going."

I held his rough hand in both of mine. "I love our life together. I love stepping outside in the morning and being able to see for miles. I love having so much space to spread out without anyone being able to see me or what I'm doing. And I love going to sleep next to you every night."

Ray lifted my hand to his lips, leaving a kiss on the back of my palm and then my fingertips laced through his. "You're an amazing wife, and Zara is right. You're going to make one hell of a mom."

TEN

ZARA

WE SPENT the rest of the day working on making the website for our fundraiser. We called it Saving Waldo and talked about wanting to keep Waldo's Diner as a part of our community for generations to come. Karen and Chester had the potential to leave that kind of legacy, if given the opportunity.

While Kai worked on the website and Ronan wrote the copy, the rest of us worked on compiling a list of donors to call or email for contributions. It was late, and my back was hurting from sitting on the couch or the floor, hunched over a laptop, when people started going home.

When Ronan walked the last of our friends out the door, I pushed my computer off my lap and groaned, lying back on the couch. "I'm exhausted."

Ronan came to the couch and sat by me, dropping a kiss on my forehead. "I love that you're doing this."

I looked up at him, feeling somewhat guilty. "I know you don't have the best memories there, but I do. I can't help remembering all the times Mom and I went there for Saturday breakfasts or all the milkshakes the girls and I had after football games."

He reached up and ran his thumb over my cheek. "It's all a part of our story. The sad parts matter too."

I closed my eyes against his touch. "I feel like I'm in a happy part, with you. Busy, but happy." When I opened my eyes again, he was smiling, something sparking in his dark eyes. "What's that look for?" I asked.

"Come on." He took my hands, pulling me up from the couch.

I moved slowly, saying, "You better be taking me to bed, to sleep."

He laughed. "As if. Put on your boots."

"My boots?"

He nodded, and I went back to my closet, getting my leather motorcycle boots. I slipped them on and went back to the living room, seeing Ronan standing with his helmet resting under his arm.

Damn, did he look hot like that, his pale skin contrasting his dark eyes and hair. His arm muscles flexing slightly against the helmet.

"Ready?" he asked.

I reached for my extra helmet in his free hand. "Let's go."

We took the elevator down and went to the parking garage. In the dim lights, it gleamed dangerously like adventure. I remembered back to all those years ago when I was leaving Ryde Alexander outside a club and a stranger offered me a ride.

I would say I had no idea how much he'd come to mean to me, but there had always been something special about Ronan—a spark I couldn't deny or ignore.

He got on the bike first, and I climbed behind him, wrapping my arms around his solid core. The bike vibrated underneath me as he kicked it to life, and the engine roared as he sped out of the parking garage and into the cool night air.

We wove through traffic until we made it to the highway along the coast, and we drove through the dark night, stars twinkling above us in the sky. It had been so long, I just savored the feeling of my arms around his waist, the warmth of his back against my cheek, the wind flying around us.

But then he slowed at a turnoff to a little-traveled beach. My eyes widened as I recognized it. This was where we had our first time. I grinned, wondering if he wanted to recreate the moment.

He stopped the bike at the end of the gravel lot and turned it off. I stepped off the bike, steadying my legs and taking off my helmet. When he looked at me, there was a gleam in his dark eyes. "Do you remember this place?"

"How could I forget?"

He took me in his arms and kissed me slowly, our breaths mingling with the breeze. Moments later, he pulled back and looked over the ocean, a million thoughts reflected in his eyes. I was used to his introspection now, used to the fact that he'd think hundreds of things before telling me one. I always knew that thought mattered more than anything for him to share it with me.

He turned to me now, and I held my breath, waiting for his thoughts.

"I've always promised myself that when I started a family, it would be the forever kind."

I nodded slightly.

"You're kind, smart, stubborn as hell, and you

love harder than anyone I've ever met. Zara, *you* are my family." He reached into his pocket before lowering to his knee.

I covered my mouth with both of my hands while my brain screamed. HE'S PROPOSING. I'd never expected it. Always been happy with his loyalty, knowing he'd always be at my side.

But now he opened the box, a black stone shimmering on a silver band, illuminated by the moon above.

"I want you to be my wife, and I want everyone to know that we are our forever family." He smiled, light glinting in each of his features. "I don't care where the wedding is, but I want the reception to be at Waldo's Diner, because I know you're going to do this, and I'm lucky as hell to be along for the ride."

I wrapped my arms around his neck, kissing him with tears streaming down my cheeks. "Of course I'll be your wife, Ronan. It was always forever with you."

The next morning, as I drove to Chester's house, I couldn't stop glancing at the ring on my finger wrapped around the steering wheel. In the daytime, there was so much depth to the black diamond surrounded by traditional diamonds. Ronan said a traditional ring hadn't felt right, not for us, and I could agree more.

After this, we were meeting Dad for lunch at Halfway Café, and I couldn't wait to tell him, because he'd hinted more than once that Ronan and I should be married since we were living together. He would be thrilled that his traditional values had rubbed off on us. Besides, he loved Ronan as the son he never had.

My phone notified me that Chester's house was approaching on the right, but I wouldn't have needed that notification because I could see Ginger's truck and Callie's mom's minivan parked along the street. Beckett's car was there too.

I pulled up behind their vehicles and walked up to where everyone was talking in the driveway while Ginger set up her recording equipment. Callie was reading off a piece of paper to Chester and Karen, and as I got closer, I realized she was prepping them with the questions she would ask.

"Hi there!" I said with a wave.

Chester extended his arms for a hug. "It's so good to see you. How's life in the big city treating you?"

"Fabulous," I said, releasing him to give Karen a hug as well. "In fact..."

I held out my hand to show them my engagement ring.

"Well, I'll be damned," Chester said, but that was quickly drowned out by Callie's squeal.

"You're getting married!" she cried.

"Congratulations!" Ginger said. "Did Ray and I miss the proposal?"

I shook my head. "After everyone left, he took me to a spot we always used to go and popped the question." I grinned at Chester. "He said he wants to have the reception at Waldo's when it gets rebuilt."

He rubbed his hands together. "We better get rolling then."

Ginger held up her camera. "I'm ready when you are."

ELEVEN

RORY

FOR THE LAST couple of years, I'd created a sort of spring break tradition. I'd sleep in on Monday morning, then lie in bed all day watching romance movies without answering text messages or having my name called by students or cleaning up paint splatters or water spills. For the next few days, I'd enjoy my time off with projects at home, visiting my parents or my brother, and hang out with friends as much as I could.

This year was different. We had to raise over half a million dollars and put an offer in on a commercial piece of land. After that, the process to rebuild Waldo's Diner would begin. But now, we were all driving to Callie's parents' house to review the video Ginger put together and get the fundraising page up and running.

Beckett brushed his teeth on his side of the sink while I applied foundation to my skin. We didn't talk much in the morning because my PCOS left me feeling really fatigued upon waking, but this silence felt heavy. And I had to wonder... Would just the two of us be enough?

This year? Five years from now? What about fifty years from now?

He spit into the sink and rinsed his mouth. "Excited to hang out with the girls today?"

I nodded, capping my foundation bottle, then moving on to contour. "You sent them all your photos, right?"

"Ginger should have them all, but you can call me if you need anything else. I'll be in the office all day today."

"Okay," I replied. I finished blending the colors on my cheeks and then put the sponge down and began drawing eyeliner above my lashes.

Beckett folded his arms across his chest and leaned back against his countertop. "My dad wants to know if we're on for Thursday night dinner. I told him I wasn't sure since we were fundraising."

"I'm calling the theater today to set up a showing time. I'll let you know after."

"Thanks." He waited for me to cap my eyeliner, then dropped a kiss on my cheek. "I know it's been a hard few days, but I just want to say I'm really proud of you. Throwing yourself into this project—it's like I have my Rory back."

I managed a smile despite the tears prickling my eyes. And because I didn't have it in me to speak, I kissed his lips and uttered a quick, "Have a good day."

It was like there were these parts to the puzzle of my life. Individually, they were fine—until they came together and the missing piece was glaring back at me.

A glance at my phone told me it was time to leave, so I finished up and grabbed my packed lunch from the fridge. I'd read all about certain foods to boost your fertility and always had spearmint tea in a bottle since it was supposed to help with the main trademark of PCOS, elevated testosterone levels.

I took it all out of the house and drove toward Callie's family home. Even though it had been quite some time, I knew the path by heart. We'd had so many good memories there, and the closer I got, the warmer my heart felt until I was knocking on the door and Callie's sweet mom was greeting me with a warm smile on her face.

"It's so great to see you, Rory!" She gave me a tight squeeze. "I have everything set up for you all downstairs. There are a couple of folding tables, some power cords, of course snacks and drinks, and you remember where the restrooms are." She stopped at the top of the stairs.

"Thank you so much," I said. "It feels like coming back home."

"It certainly reminds me of good times. Maybe someday you'll all be coming over with your kiddos and having play dates." She lowered her voice. "If we can talk Callie into moving back."

My throat felt tight, so I swallowed before saying, "I'd like that very much."

She gave me a smile before turning away, and I took the stairs down to find Callie and Ginger. Everyone else had to go to their jobs, so it would be the three of us working most of the day until they got off.

But then my eyes fell on the calf, standing in the backyard. "Oh my gosh, you brought Oscar over?"

Callie grinned as Ginger nodded.

"How's he doing?" I asked, walking closer to the

window.

"Great," Ginger said. "He's been taking fluids well and feeding decently. We're going to put him out with his mom tomorrow. Ray checked, and she's producing milk, but if he's not feeding well, we'll keep him as a bucket calf."

"Bucket calf?" I asked.

Ginger nodded. "Basically bottle-feed him until he's old enough to be weaned and go back with the rest of the herd."

"Wow," I said, walking back to the table. "So, where are we starting today?"

Callie tapped on her laptop, pulling up an Excel sheet with lines of several colors. "We need to review the video, upload it to the website, and call the theater to schedule a special screening. Then we'll start our email and phone campaign while one of us designs and prints flyers. We'll need to get those out around town as soon as possible."

Ginger nodded. "I'll pull up the video. Can I cast it to your TV?"

"Sure," Callie said going to get the remote.

I went to the couch and sat down, excited to see what she'd been working on. In a few minutes, soft music played as white text showed over a black screen.

. . .

Chester and Karen Sutherland are the owners of Waldo's Diner.

For the last 30 years, the diner has been a staple to our community.

After-game milkshakes.

Brunch dates with friends.

Family dinners.

Coffee chats.

But on March 10, it burned down.

Leaving them without the business they rented.

And leaving us without the value they gave.

My eyes were already watering, and I hadn't even heard Chester or Karen speak yet.

Now a corporation is trying to purchase the land from Chester and Karen's landlords, meaning Waldo's Diner could be gone... forever.

. . .

Chester and Karen came on the screen, sitting on their front porch and speaking into the camera. Chester told the story of retiring and then learning the restaurant needed a new owner. Then they shared parts of the story I hadn't known.

For years, he and Karen had been estranged from their daughter, so they threw themselves into running the diner and volunteering, trying to fill the hole of her absence. They'd been creating a family to replace what they were so desperately missing.

Then Beckett got on camera. I raised my eyebrows, because I hadn't been expecting that, but I set my surprise aside to listen.

"I've been coming to Waldo's Diner for as long as I can remember. My dad used to take me out every Saturday morning for breakfast. Chester would greet us on the way in, and he always gave me a quarter for the gumball machine—before and after the meal." Beckett chuckled endearingly. "Then, as I got older, it became 'the' place. We celebrated there after football games, hung out after dances, and took our girls on dates. Back when my wife and I were first seeing each other, it was a favorite place to go. I'd hate to rid our future children of that privilege."

My heart melted, and I wiped at my eyes. Callie

gently patted my shoulder, but the tears kept coming. Beckett was still planning for us to have a family. That meant the world to me.

Then one of my favorite waitresses, Betty, came on and talked about how Chester and Karen had been a second family to her. They'd given her a flexible schedule while caring for her mom and even paid her paycheck for an entire month after her mom passed to give her time to grieve.

Callie went on camera and talked about how amazing it was to walk into a place and be greeted so kindly by Chester and the staff, especially when you were bullied at school. She said it had been one of the brightest parts of her day.

I reached over and squeezed her hand.

At the end of the film, the white text said...

We want to buy the property and give it to the rightful owners, Chester and Karen Sutherland, so they can continue giving the community an extra place to call home...

Any support, big or small, can help save Waldo's Diner.

. . .

As captions rolled down the screen, Callie and I clapped loudly.

"It's amazing, Ginger!" I said. "I can't believe you put it together so quickly."

Ginger held up her coffee. "It's been a couple of sleepless nights. And there aren't fancy transitions or anything, but I'm not sure we needed them in this case."

Callie wiped at her eyes. "It's brilliant, Ging. I really think we can do this."

Ginger grinned. "Let's do it then."

While she got to work adding the video to the website for each donor to watch, I called the movie theater and eventually found my way to a manager. Turns out he took his daughter to Waldo's every Friday night and was glad to offer us a showing during a prime time on Friday evening. All that was left to do was get the flyers designed and printed.

Easy peasy.

That is, until Aiden called me.

I answered and said, "Hey, what's up?"

"I hate to do this to you on spring break, but is there any way you could pick up Casen and watch him until I get off work? Our babysitter called in sick, and everyone else is busy."

"I'm glad I was your last resort," I retorted.

He let out a laugh. "Is that a yes? You'd really be saving our bacon, Rory."

"Of course. Do I need to come get him?"

"I'm already driving. Can I drop him at your place?"

"Hold on." I covered the phone and asked if it was okay for Casen to come over. They said of course, and soon, I was meeting Aiden at the front door with my nephew.

Casen made sweet cooing sounds as he reached for me, and I held his squishy body close to me.

With his tie askew, Aiden handed me the diaper bag, a lunch box, and the baby carrier, and then set a pack and play on the ground. "That should be everything you need."

"How did you carry all of that?" I asked, looking from Casen to my brother.

"You grow an extra hand when you're a parent. You'll see one day."

"Right," I said with half a smile. I picked up Casen's arm and waved at Aiden. "Have a good day at work, Daddy!"

Aiden gave me a grateful smile and then drove away.

TWELVE
CALLIE

WE ALL TOOK turns holding Casen while looking over the flyer Ginger designed using a template online. But soon we were piling into Rory's car and heading to the print shop to pick up a case of flyers.

I sat in the back with him, entertaining him as we drove. "He's the sweetest baby," I said, rattling the toy in front of his fingers.

Rory said, "The best. And I love his hazel eyes. He reminds me so much of Aiden."

I looked at him, wondering what a mix of Carson and me would look like. Maybe someday I'd find out, but I couldn't help feeling like I had more to accomplish before starting a family.

Ginger turned to look at me, then Rory, and said, "I have a confession to make."

"What's that?" Rory asked.

"Ray and I are trying for a baby."

My jaw dropped, half surprised for her and half hurting for Rory. I knew Rory and Beckett had been struggling with infertility for at least a year, but as far as I knew, Beckett had only told Carson about it. I wasn't supposed to know, which made navigating these waters even trickier.

Rory replied first, saying, "Congratulations!"

Did Ginger notice the strain in her voice? The way her excitement felt forced?

"That is wonderful," I agreed. "How did you guys decide it was time?"

Ginger smiled. "Well, I know Ray is going to be an amazing dad. And we have that great house on the ranch to raise a family in. I have some steady clients, so we don't have to worry about money. But mostly, it was just a feeling that it's the right time, honestly."

I nodded as if I understood. "You're going to be great parents, and your kids will love having all that room to play on the farm. Have you told your parents?"

Ginger shook her head. "Things are still kind of strained with my parents. And they're so busy with the twins graduating high school while filming for that show in LA."

Rory frowned. "I thought you and your parents were doing so much better."

Ginger rolled her eyes. "We were, until my mom decided to throw away every single cleaning supply in my house and swap it with her own. I swear, she won't accept that I'm an adult and can make my own choices. She still texts me every month to make sure I have all my prescriptions filled."

Rory turned into the print shop parking lot, and Ginger said, "I'll go grab the flyers." She got out, leaving Rory and me alone with Casen, and because I couldn't take the pain I felt radiating from Rory, I said, "I know I'm not supposed to know, but Carson told me you and Beckett are having a hard time getting pregnant. I'm so sorry, but I know you and Beckett are going to make great parents someday too."

I watched in the rearview mirror as Rory blinked quickly, then wiped at her eyes. "I'm not surprised Beckett told Carson. We keep hoping for a miracle," she said. "But every month, it doesn't happen. And Beckett's tired of trying. It feels impossible."

I reached up and rubbed her shoulder. "I'm here for you."

She touched my hand gently, then let go. "Thank you."

"Of course," I said quietly.

She didn't speak for a few moments, gathering herself before Ginger returned to the car.

Ginger came out of the store carrying a massive cardboard box, then set it in the trunk. When she got back into the car, she said, "A thousand flyers are way heavier than I thought they would be."

Rory laughed slightly. "Looks like we've got our work cut out for us."

We decided to split up, dropping Ginger off on the north end of Main Street and then driving to the south side of Main Street to canvass businesses. Rory used a baby carrier to strap Casen to her front, and I held an armful of flyers as we made our way down the right side of the street.

I glanced over at Rory adjusting Casen's sun hat and smiled. "You're a natural with a baby."

She grinned at Casen, gently tickling his shoulders. "You're just an easy little babe to be with, aren't you!"

He let out a raspy giggle, and I grinned. "If nothing else, he'll make us look more sympathetic."

Rory laughed. "Casey and Aiden would love that, showing off their baby for extra donations."

I laughed too, making Casen smile at the both of us. "He just needs a little sign and a puppy." My eyes widened. "Oh my gosh, we should get a puppy from the shelter to go with us tomorrow!"

"Brilliant," Rory said, turning to the first business on our right. "Are we ready?"

I nodded, and she said, "For Waldo's Diner," before opening the door.

I got out of the shower, feeling all the thirty-thousand steps my watch said I walked today. Between taking turns carrying Casen on our fronts and then walking in and out of every business to post our flyers, I was completely worn out, and we had only put up four hundred. That left more than half to distribute.

Tonight, Beckett and Kai were sending emails, but our tracker on the website was already going up. We had raised eight thousand dollars today, just by speaking with business owners and people on the sidewalk who loved Waldo's Diner.

But compared to half a million dollars, it was

less than half a drop in the bucket. We needed more, and we needed it fast. I could only hope the email campaign went well tonight and that our fundraising phone calls tomorrow would go even better.

I put my hair up in the yellow shower cap I kept at home and applied some medicated lotion at the base of my neck. Even though I'd only been off my job for a week, my psoriasis was already getting better. That job had taken a toll on not only my mind, but my body as well. I felt happier, freer, in Emerson than I ever had in North Carolina. The only thing missing was the love of my life.

I got out my phone and dialed his number for a video call, then sat cross-legged on my bed while waiting for him to answer.

His face appeared on the screen, and my heart instantly settled. "Hi, beautiful," he said, his voice warming me from the inside out.

"I miss you," I said, taking in all his features. His bright blue eyes, the blonder tips at the ends of his hair, his smile that crinkled the corners of his eyes. He must have been sitting outside, because I could see the sun on his face, making his skin a perfect shade of gold.

"I miss you too. Tell me all about your day so I can pretend I was there."

I smiled, adjusting my grip on the phone, and shared all about the documentary and passing out flyers and hanging out with Casen all day. "It was a really good day. The only thing missing was you."

The doorbell rang, and I said, "Mom and Dad'll get it."

Carson nodded. "So what about jobs? Have you given that any thought?"

I shrugged. "I'd work at a shelter again, but volunteering doesn't exactly pay the bills, and there's no way I'm going back to school to become a vet, especially with how much they suffer with their mental health."

"I get that," he said.

The doorbell rang again, and I said, "Hold on. Mom! Dad! Are you getting that?" When they didn't reply, I said, "Hang on," to Carson and got out of bed to go to the door.

"Sure," Carson said.

I walked down the stairs and went to the front door, a little annoyed at Mom and Dad for not answering, but I didn't see them in the living room or the dining room. Where the heck did they go?

I pulled the door open, hoping it was someone

planning to leave quickly, but when I saw who it was, I dropped my phone.

"Carson!" I cried and jumped into his arms.

He held me tight, his chest shaking with his laughter. "Hi, baby girl."

I stepped back, taking his face and then his arms in my hands. "Oh my gosh, you're here! What are you doing here? Don't you have to work?"

"I couldn't miss this," he said.

"But our rent, and my job——"

"We have a lot to talk about," he said, "but first..." He drew me closer and planted a slow kiss on my lips. I loved his taste, his scent, the careful way he held me, like I was the most precious thing in the world. My heart beat in tune with his until we parted.

I stared up at him a moment, just loving the sight of his blue eyes on mine, and then I said, "Want to go to the greenbelt, like old times?"

He nodded. We held hands as we walked through the house, out the back sliding door, and across our lawn to the gate at the back of the yard. The grassy greenbelt that wound through our neighborhood spread before us, and we walked around the curve until we reached the park where we'd met. The same swings were still there—the ones we'd first competed on to see who could go higher.

Smiling at the memory, I took the one I had all those years ago. It was tighter fit now, the chains digging into my sides, but I didn't mind all that much. "Tell me, what do we have to talk about?"

He looked over at me. "Clary's moving—her whole family. Josh got a job in Florida near Mom, and they're set to move at the end of the month."

My heart sank. The only thing that had made North Carolina seem like home was having Carson's family there. "We can't stay there by ourselves." It was a selfish thing to say, and I knew it, but after two years of giving all of myself away for a job, there wasn't all that much left to give.

"I know," he said. "That's why I quit."

My eyes widened. "You what?"

"I talked to Lee after you left and told him that I've loved working there, but it was time to move back home. He said he understood, and that was that."

"Seriously? What about your last two weeks?"

"I'm taking this week off to help with Waldo's, and then I'll finish up the month at the gym, training my replacement. I already talked to our landlord. They wanted to raise the rent anyway, so they're letting us out a few months early. We're homeless."

It was the best news I'd heard in such a long time. I got off the swing and hugged him. "Are you sure about this?"

He pulled back, resting his forehead against mine. "I'm sure about you. I know you'll be happier here, surrounded by people you love, and we'll figure out the rest. Together."

THIRTEEN
JORDAN

I STOOD on a pedestal while a seamstress plucked
at my deep purple bridesmaid dress. Mom sat on a
nearby chair, chatting with me, while my soon-to-be
stepsister sat on her phone with an annoyed look on
her face.

To be fair, I didn't want to be here either, but for
completely different reasons. First of all, I should
have been helping the girls canvass the town since I
had a day off and could help. Secondly, I'd never, in
my life, worn a tailored dress. I'd always gotten my
dresses right off the rack and mostly in second-hand
shops.

But now?

This dress was going to be made for my body.

And that took time, talent, and a lot of money that my mom's fiancé was paying for.

"That looks lovely on you," Mom said, staring up at me, her eyes shining with tears.

My stomach fell with guilt. Could she tell what I had just been thinking? We should both be happy right now. "What's wrong, Mom?"

She shook her head, wiping at her eyes. "I was just thinking how I wish I could have gotten you special prom dresses like this."

I wished I could go hug her, but since I was covered in pins, it wasn't exactly an option. "You gave me everything I needed, Mom," I said. "Having you as my best friend was the greatest gift."

She pressed at the corners of her eyes, trying to stem the tears. "You worked your whole life when you should have been having fun."

Now Arabella was trying not to show she was staring at us, her thumbs still on her phone.

I opened my mouth to reply, but I... couldn't. Mom was right. I remembered after Juana died and Dad left, she'd brought me along on cleaning jobs until I was old enough to stay home by myself. Then I was expected to keep house, cook meals on a budget, clean our apartment. And then, in high school, I was working alongside her again, filling the gap in her new business. I loved her, but I wondered if that was part of the reason I had so much trouble with work-life balance now. I'd only ever known work, never done much for personal pleasure until I met Kai, and I still got itchy after a few days of vacation.

The seamstress, Tiana, stepped back and said, "I think this dress more than makes up for it. Look at yourself, Jordan."

At her urging, I turned and looked at myself in the mirror, my mouth falling open. This evening gown transformed me from a tired resident to a beautiful, powerful woman. The silky dress had long sleeves, a neckline that drew across my collarbone to keep my breasts from stealing the focus, and then the dress nipped in at the waist, putting my curves on display. In this dress, I looked every bit the billionaire's girlfriend instead of regular old me.

Mom came and stood beside me, watching my reflection in the mirror. "It's beautiful, *mija*."

I reached for her hand, holding it tight. "It will be nothing compared to you on your wedding day." It was coming up soon, only a month away. "But promise me, even after you marry him, it'll always be you and me against the world?"

She kissed the back of my hand and looked up at me. "Always. We'll just have some extra people on our team now."

I'd wanted her to tell me it would always be the same, but she was right. Our world was changing, growing. It wasn't just us in our mother/daughter bubble anymore.

Tiana finished with her measurements and pins and then helped me out of the gown. Now it was my future stepsister's turn, and she required a lot more of my mother's attention. And a lot more time as they made sure it fit her well.

"Hey, sorry to interrupt," I said to them, "but I need to go meet Kai. We're supposed to have lunch together."

Mom gave me a hug and said, "I love you. Text me the date for the documentary showing. I want to make sure it's on Javier's calendar too so we can both be there to support you."

"I will," I promised. I left the dress shop and drove from Brentwood to downtown Emerson, where I was supposed to meet Kai. Even though things had been rough between us, I was excited to spend more time with him. And now that I under-stood a little more why relaxing felt so uncomfortable, maybe it would be easier to practice relaxing with him.

When I reached the address, I was confused. It was on a side street near Main, but I wasn't sure what restaurant was nearby that he'd like. I parked next to his car, and he got out, waiting for me on the sidewalk.

And damn, did he look good in his khakis with his dark shirt rolled at the sleeves. I got out and smiled at him. "You look amazing."

His smile seemed strained. "You too." He kissed my cheek.

Looking around, I asked. "Where's the restaurant?"

"Actually, I was hoping we could do something else." I would have thought he had a surprise for me if it weren't for the pinch to his lips and the tension in his shoulders.

"What's going on?" I asked.

He took my hand and walked me down the sidewalk a little farther to a glass door in the brick building with gold letters printed above the handle.

Rielle Taylor, Family and Couples Counselor, LMHC

I stared from the door to Kai, confusion constricting my chest. "What are we doing here?"

He spoke quickly, his hand tight on mine. "Jordan, I think we need counseling."

I raised my eyebrows. "And you didn't think to tell me?"

"I didn't think you'd come."

"Damn right I wouldn't have come. How can we fix a problem I don't even know exists?"

"Jordan..." He took my other hand in his so he was holding both of mine, and it took all I had not to pull away. "How can I tell you I have a problem if we never have time to talk about it and it's always brushed under the rug? I love you, and I want to be with you, but for that to work for both of us, we need to get on the same page."

My eyes stung, and I looked away, not sure I could speak over the anger and grief flooding my system.

"Please, do this for me?" he asked.

I met his eyes again. The beautiful dark almond eyes I'd lost myself in so much as a teen. If I was being honest with myself, he was right. We'd drifted apart, caught up in work and business, and if I wanted to find the happiness my mom had found for herself... something had to change.

I nodded slowly, and Kai said, "Thank you," before opening the door.

We checked in, and soon a woman with clear glasses and blond hair was telling us to come back to her office.

The first thing I noticed was how trendy it was. With a modern gray couch and plants hanging in the window, it was both sleek and inviting—as inviting as a therapy office could be. I'd gone to therapy once a month for the last few years, and it wasn't my idea of fun, talking about my problems. I just hoped this would be less painful.

"I'm Rielle," she said. "I do work with individuals and families, but my main specialty is couples. Can you tell me what brought you in today?"

I looked at Kai, my jaw tight. This had been his idea entirely.

"Jordan and I have been together since our senior year of high school. We've always been pretty solid until the last year or so. Jordan's busy with med school, and I have a software start-up. Right now it feels like..." He let out a sigh, not meeting my eyes. "It feels like we're on different planes, even when we're side by side."

His words were a knife to my heart.

Rielle looked at me, her eyes a piercing blue behind her glasses. "Would you agree with that, Jordan?"

I didn't want to. God knows I didn't want to. But I did. "I do."

She nodded quietly as I wiped my eyes.

"What I find helpful in couples counseling," she said, "is if we start with a goal in mind. Do you have any ideas?"

I glanced toward Kai, waiting for his answer.

He said, "I want to marry Jordan, but I don't want our lives to look like this."

Rielle wrote on a legal pad, then said, "If I'm understanding you right, Kai, you want to know if this is a relationship to continue."

Kai nodded, but he might as well have crushed my heart in his hands.

"And Jordan?" she asked.

The words came out of my mouth before I had even thought them. "I want to feel supported in my dreams." Surely he could come to understand what it was like for me to work so many hours and still try to maintain a relationship with him, my mom, and my friends.

Rielle nodded. "That's a great goal, Jordan." She finished writing in her notebook and then looked at both of us. "Coming to counseling is a commitment. It may require you to rearrange your schedule, face some uncomfortable feelings, and be brutally honest with each other... and yourselves. But if you can stick with it, in the end, your relationship and your respect for each other will be stronger than it's ever been before."

I sat quietly, wondering how on earth I could feel strong when I'd never felt more broken.

She helped us schedule a time for the next week, and then Kai and I left the office side by side, but not touching at all. Outside of the softly lit building, the sun felt bright, strong, punishing.

We faced each other on the sidewalk, neither of us speaking for a moment.

"Jordan," Kai began, but I held up my hand.

"How dare you," I said, my jaw trembling.

"Jordan, I—"

I shook my head. "You bombarded me with therapy that I didn't ask for, and then you told a complete stranger that you don't know if you want to be with me long-term. Is that it? Shape up or ship out?"

"That's not what I was trying to do. I love you, Jordan, and you've barely made any time for me. Can't you see that?"

The desperate look in his eyes nearly tore me in two. "I loved that you always believed in me, Kai. From the moment you met me, you knew I had big dreams. That I wanted to be a doctor. And now that I'm almost done with med school, you tell me it's all too much? That we're growing apart? Of course we are! We don't go to the same school every day! We have careers, bills to pay, a home to manage, and life to worry about."

"But that's the thing, Jordan. You are my life. I'm only a part of yours."

I blinked rapidly, trying to stop the flow of tears before saying, "Apparently not for long." I shook my head. "You can get 'lunch' by yourself."

THERE WAS a map of the city spread out on the table in Callie's basement. Rory, Callie, Carson, and I stood over it, highlighting the areas like a crew of pirates searching for gold. We cross-referenced the highlighted sections assigned to us with the maps on our phones, making sure we were hitting every last strip mall and office park.

It was nice, having Carson here. Callie seemed so much lighter with him around, and he certainly lightened our workload. Which seemed heavy as ever with each business added to the list.

Rory looked up at me and said, "You're good to ask your parents for a donation, right?"

I didn't really want to speak with them, but sending someone else in my place would only make things more strained, and not asking them at all would hurt our cause. So I nodded and decided to "cowgirl up" as Ray's sister, Laura, liked to say. She was fearless—on a horse, around cattle, in life. But me? Not so much. I wasn't brave like Laura or Cori...

Maybe that was my ticket out, I thought to myself... I could ask Cori to speak with our parents, and I could use the excuse of being busy with the farm for my continued silence.

We were about to go our separate ways when the front door opened. We all looked up and saw Jordan coming down the stairs.

I said, "I thought you were grabbing a long lunch with Kai."

She shook her head. "That was a joke."

The other four of us gave each other a look because we could see her emotions on her face no matter how strong she tried to be.

"What's going on?" Callie asked.

Jordan shook her head, blinking quickly. "Kai surprised me with couples therapy."

I covered my mouth, shocked. "Surprised you? What do you mean?"

"We met on Main Street for lunch, I *thought*, but then we walked into a therapist's office, and he basically told her that he doesn't want to be with me anymore if I don't focus more on our relationship instead of work. It was like he wanted to get married or break up; there was no in between."

Rory had her hands over her mouth, and Callie looked so sad. My heart was breaking for her after everything she had worked for. I knew she loved him, but I could see Kai's point of view as well. It seemed like since she'd gotten so wrapped up in school and work, we had seen and heard less and less from her. Sometimes she had a hard time prioritizing her life when she went all in on something.

"Do you think you two will figure it out?" Carson asked, sympathy clear in his features.

She shrugged. "Our therapist seems to think we can, but right now, I don't know if I want to."

The honesty in her words broke my heart. I had always thought how cool it was that the five of us were still with our high school sweethearts, living happily ever after. But I knew that's not what happens for most people. And society liked to remind me of that. What Ray and I shared, it was rare and special. And if Jordan and Kai broke up, they wouldn't be in the minority. But that didn't mean I wanted that pain for my friend.

"Do you want to talk about it?" Callie asked.

She shook her head. "I want to help."

So I said, "Why don't you come along with me?"

She nodded quietly, and on our way out the door, she decided she wanted to take her own car and drive home after our campaigning. As we drove to the first business park, I called my sister Cori.

She answered after a few rings. "What's up?"

"I need a favor. We're trying to canvass the town with our flyers for the fundraiser, and I was wondering if you would be willing to call Mom and Dad and maybe hitting up the other businesses in that area?"

She was quiet for a moment. "Are you sure you can't do it? I have three showings today, and I'm trying to get a hold of Des to share on her social..."

"That's exciting! I didn't even think of calling Des," I said. But I could tell there was more to her refusal. "Are you sure you can't call Mom for me?"

"I just really don't want to get in the middle of it," she said.

"You don't want to get in the middle of what?" I asked, already knowing what I meant. If I could feel the distance, mom could probably feel it too.

"Mom misses you, Ging."

I let out a sigh. "Look, it's just easier if you do it."

"That doesn't mean that it's the right thing," she said.

"But they—"

"I *know* our parents have made a lot of mistakes, especially when it comes to their relationship with you, but I think you'd be surprised how they'd show up for you if you had an honest conversation with them."

"Okay, thanks," I said before hanging up, tears threatening to fall.

I didn't really want to belabor the point. Cori didn't understand because she had always been healthy and safe in our parents' eyes. *I* had been the one who they hovered over, the one who made a mistake with my medication, the one who was never responsible enough to make my own choices. And even though they had come around to me dating and eventually marrying a rancher using conventional practices, there were still sore points between us.

I wanted to focus on Chester and Karen and getting the diner back for them. So I parked in an office park and waited for Jordan to stop her car beside mine. We got out and started knocking. The work was monotonous and draining, especially when someone slammed a door in our face or pointed at a no soliciting sign we missed rather than speaking with us. But then there were the people who were supportive. They offered kind smiles and donations and excitement to watch the film we'd created.

We were making a difference, one dollar, one donation, one notch up the thermometer on the website at a time.

When we had knocked on every door and left flyers with every person who hadn't answered, we went back out to the parking lot, and Jordan said, "Do you want to hit Ripe next? It's just a half a mile that way, right?"

I groaned internally, knowing that the longer I avoided my parents, the longer I'd let them have power over me. So I simply nodded and said, "Let's go."

We drove to Ripe, and I stood next to my car, staring at the sign with the twisting letters and the yellow banana, thinking about how much time I'd spent in this very store.

I saw my dad's car parked a few rows away, and even though we'd always gotten on a little better than my mom and me, he had always accepted her behaviors. In my mind, that was just as bad.

Jordan patted my back. "I'll go to the other businesses while you say hi to your parents?"

I nodded and walked toward the sliding doors. As soon as I stepped through, the cashier who had always worked there, Janet, gave me a grin and said, "It's so good to see you, kid. How are you doing?"

"Pretty good," I said back, already feeling a little bit more comfortable. I would have chatted longer, but she was still working with a customer, so I walked toward the office, expecting to find my dad.

Instead, I saw the assistant manager who Dad was training to take over so he could actually take a vacation sometime. "Hey, Knox," I said. I still couldn't believe the cute college guy I'd stocked shelves with was still around. Although he was a cute man now. "Do you know where my dad is?"

"Hey," he replied with a grin. "I'm pretty sure he's in the back, breaking down some boxes."

I nodded. Of course he was. Dad was never one to sit back while everyone else did the hard work.

I chatted with Knox a little longer, then walked toward the back of the store to the room where they kept all of the extra shipments. Dad was doing exactly what Knox said, using a box cutter to break down boxes, a bead of sweat growing on his forehead.

"Hi, Dad," I said. I didn't know what else to say.

He looked up at me, surprise on his face. "Ginger, what are you doing here?"

Awkwardly, I held up a flyer. "My friends and I are trying to help out Waldo's Diner. You heard it burned down, right?"

"Yeah. Tragic, really." He folded up his box cutter and slipped it in his pocket, wiping his forehead as he walked toward me to pick up the flyer. He looked from it to me for a moment, and I knew he was waiting for me to speak.

"Dad, we were hoping you would be one of the donors or that the store would donate to help save the diner. We're using the funds to buy back the plot of land and build another diner there."

He ran his hand over his beard, quiet for a moment. "You came here for money."

It wasn't a question. "It's tax deductible," I said. As if that helped.

He folded the flyer in half and then quarters. "Your mom's beside herself that you haven't called her or answered her calls since you and Ray moved into your new place. She's worried you're gonna have grandbabies without telling her."

Guilt settled in my stomach like a lead brick. Because that was exactly what we were doing. Or trying to, at least. Not that I would ever admit that to Mom. I just didn't want my child to feel the same way I had growing up. And even though I was excited to be a mom, I didn't want my own mom to make *me* feel inadequate.

"Dad, what she did was not okay. She treats me like a child."

He frowned. "You know your mother always has the best intentions."

"Intentions don't matter when someone says they're hurt," I replied.

"A great conversation to have with her." He turned back to the boxes, slipping the folded paper in his back pocket. "My checkbook's at home, and we've been wanting to donate $10,000 to a charitable cause to help with our taxes this year, but it's not happening until you sort things out with your mom."

My anger made my face hot. "That's it? You're blackmailing me?"

He replied with a small smile and a shrug. "I'd hardly call that blackmail. Now if I got out some of your baby pictures and threatened to share them with everyone in town, it would be a different story."

I turned around to walk out of the store before I said something stupid and was nearly out the door when I heard my phone ring. I pulled it out of my purse, seeing Ray's name on the screen.

When I answered, he said, "I've got some bad news."

My heart stalled, and I stopped on the sidewalk outside, shielding my eyes from the sun. "What do you mean, bad news?"

"We tried to put Oscar back with his mom, but she's not giving him any milk. So it's looking like we'll have to sell him."

That was the last straw. Tears formed in my eyes. "What will happen to him?"

"Some kid'll probably get him as a bucket calf if a feedlot doesn't take him."

Just the thought of my Oscar going somewhere else broke my heart more. "That's not happening."

"Do you have another idea?" he asked.

"Yeah," I replied. "He's mine."

FIFTEEN

ZARA

IT WAS GETTING LATE. Almost everyone had left the office, and I was just finishing up some paperwork on the option we were trying to do with another author. But if Ronan and I didn't leave soon, we were going to miss supper with my dad.

He wanted to take Ronan and me out to celebrate our engagement. And even though we still had plenty of doors to knock on and people to call to raise money for Waldo's Diner, we decided to take a little break. We needed to eat either way. And there was no way I would deny my father the pleasure of finally seeing me and Ronan together, engaged, when he had spent so much of my younger years trying to marry me off.

I stacked my paperwork neatly on my desk and then picked up my blazer and purse. Doing a final sweep of my office to make sure it was neat, I turned off the light, locked the door and left. The writers often worked longer than production did, especially in the drafting phase of a show, so I walked down the hallway and wasn't surprised when I still heard talking coming from the writing room.

I knocked gently on the door, and when someone called *come in*, I pushed it open. The room was a massive mess of scattered paper on the tables, whiteboards full of scribbles, and sticky notes posted on the wall. I didn't really understand the creative process, but I liked the results. I especially liked how happy it made Ronan.

The senior writer on the team, Douglas, looked at me and said, "Guess that's last call for you, Ronan."

I laughed. "My dad would be pretty upset if we missed our reservation."

"Go on," Douglas said. "We're finishing up here anyway."

Ronan nodded and then looked at him. "But I still think that the third act needs a little more, maybe a twist or something."

Douglas pulled his lips to the side in thought. "I think you're on to something."

Ronan said goodbye to Douglas and the two other writers, then packed up his messenger bag and followed me into the hallway. He put his arm around my shoulders and kissed my temple. "How was your day?"

"Good," I said. "You?"

Under his breath, he said, "Douglas is making a terrible decision with this second plot line, but it's fine." It sounded like he was still trying to convince himself of that fact.

Disagreements in the writing room weren't uncommon, and Ronan had learned over the years to pick his battles. Apparently, this was not one he wanted to fight over.

"Dad's excited to see us," I said as we neared the building exit.

"I'm looking forward to it too," Ronan said. "I feel like it's been forever since we've actually sat down and hung out with him."

"Everything's been so busy here." Story of my life. "And speaking of busy, we have another fundraiser to attend next week."

He chuckled, shaking his head. "You know, at

this rate, I feel like all the world's problems should be solved."

"You'd think," I said. "But then how else would we get together and wear fancy clothes and make new connections?"

He made a face. Ronan hated that part of the business, but he'd come to accept it as a part that was necessary for him to move ahead. Knowing the right people was just as important as doing good work.

We walked into the parking garage and found my car. He offered to drive, so I gave him the keys and got into the passenger seat, pulling out my phone to check the fundraising website.

"Oh my gosh!" I said. "Can you believe we're almost three quarters of the way there with only four days of fundraising? With the movie tomorrow, I bet we can get there!"

"I never doubted you," he replied with a grin. "You girls could rule the world."

"It's not about us. Chester and Karen created a place that people were willing to get behind. A *legacy*."

He nodded as he put the car into gear. "It makes me want to write a story about them."

I smiled over to him. "Maybe someday you will.

With pictures of the new and improved diner... Have you been working on your book lately?"

He shook his head. "But I should get back into it."

"Definitely," I said.

We drove across town to La Belle, the fancy Italian restaurant near Emerson shops, and a valet took the keys from Ronan, parking the car for us. When we walked inside, we saw Dad sitting at a table big enough for the three of us. I told the hostess we were going to meet him, and she walked us back.

At the sight of us, he stood up, grinning, and gave Ronan a big hug first. "I'm so happy to see you, bud!"

"What am I? Chopped liver?" I mumbled.

Dad laughed, drawing me into a hug. "I'm so happy for you, Zara."

"Me too," I admitted. "Ronan's definitely better than Ryde." I couldn't help the jab about the man my dad had wanted me to marry.

Dad gave me a look that said he'd expected nothing less from me and sat back down at the table. Soon, a server came over to offer us water and take our drink orders. And then Dad was asking all the questions: when we wanted to get married, where we wanted to have the wedding, who we wanted to invite.

Ronan and I shared a look, and I said, "We haven't really talked about dates or anything, only that we want to have a reception at Waldo's Diner."

"The diner?" Dad said with a chuckle. "Of course you would surprise me that way."

Ronan smiled at me. "The diner means a lot to us."

I nodded, reaching for his hand and finding a reassuring squeeze.

"Well, if you don't mind," Dad said, "I would like to help plan the ceremony. I know your mother would have been happy to see you in a traditional Indian gown."

I nodded, tears stinging my eyes at the fact that my mom wouldn't see me walking down the aisle. But that tradition, that wedding, it was something she and I could share, even if she wasn't here. I pictured dressing up in the beaded sari and having my makeup done so glamorously and then seeing the man I loved at the end of the aisle.

Ronan said, "As long as we're married at the end of the day, I don't care how it happens."

I laughed, despite my emotion. "So romantic."

But Ronan was romantic. More so than I ever

knew I desired. I had a whole book full of poems he'd written me over the years. And someday, I'd like to have it bound into a beautifully designed hard cover to have our love story wrapped within its pages.

Soon, our drinks were delivered, and the server took our orders. We talked about work and life and how Dad was enjoying his new house. The production company was doing better than ever. And even though it faltered when I was in high school, it had bounced back better than we could have ever dreamed. The profits more than paid for Dad's new house and for the penthouse apartment Ronan and I shared. And although Dad's company had put quite a bit of burden on me when I was younger by attending all the functions and even hijacking my arranged marriage, I enjoyed working with him. I loved the sense of purpose I felt going into the office and arranging a deal and networking and ultimately creating something that people everywhere would talk about. It was incredible.

At the end of our meal, Dad convinced us to pick something from the dessert tray, and as I looked at my tiramisu, he reached into a bag I hadn't noticed sitting beside him.

"Zara," he said, "there are some things that

your mother had me save for you for a time when you were ready, and now's the time for you to have this." He pulled out an envelope with yellowing paper, and I saw my name written on the front and handwriting I recognized just as well as my own.

My heart stalled. "This is for me?" I breathed.

Dad nodded. "She wanted you to have it after you got engaged."

I gently touched the crisp paper, thinking of the woman I loved, the woman who raised me until she couldn't, touching this very page and knowing that I would someday hold it even when she couldn't be around. I made to open it, but Dad said, "You should do it at home when you're ready."

Even though I was desperate to feel closer to my mom, I tucked it carefully in my purse. I couldn't quite focus on my tiramisu knowing that I had something from my mom right next to me just waiting to be opened.

At the end of our meal, Dad hugged me a second longer than usual and said goodbye. Ronan and I were quiet for a moment in the car, until I reached for the envelope and held it in my lap.

Ronan broke the silence, asking, "What do you think it is?"

"I have no idea," I replied, holding the paper. I

could feel something solid inside, not just a letter. "Can you park over there so I can open it?" I asked. I didn't know why Dad didn't want me opening it in front of him, but I couldn't wait any longer. And I knew I would need Ronan's support in that moment.

Silently, Ronan pulled into the movie theater parking lot and parked far away from the building along the curb. There was no one here, so we had some semblance of privacy.

Since it was dark, I lowered the visor and opened the flap so the lights would come on. They shined just bright enough for me to see my mom's handwriting on the page. I carefully pulled up on the envelope flap. The glue, having long since deteriorated, broke loose. I opened the envelope and first saw a gold bangle. My heart stopped as I took it in my hands, trying to feel any last trace of my mother on it, any imprint of love she may have left behind. Even if it sounded crazy, I swear I felt her warmth.

I slipped it over my wrist, a perfect fit, then I opened the letter, seeing her scrawling cursive inside the page. My eyes misted over as I read the first line.

My Dear Zara,

My, how you have grown. I may not have been there to witness it in the way that we both had wished, but I hope you know that I'm there with you for every moment and with every breath.

I asked your father to give you this letter when you were on your way to becoming married because there's so much I wish we could have talked about. So many lessons I wanted to share, but some lessons weren't appropriate for the ears of an eleven-year-old. Now that you have grown, I'd love to let you know some things that I wish I had known as a young bride.

The bangle in this envelope was the one I wore when your father proposed. Although we were in an arranged marriage, I loved him deeply and quickly. I couldn't wait to spend my life with him. He had such big dreams, and I was starstruck by them, enthralled at the idea of a future and a family with a man I loved.

Marriage is both one of the most beautiful blessings and one of life's greatest trials. And it is not necessarily marriage or the partner that makes it difficult. But the constant sacrifice and dealing with one another's wounds that bring out challenges. Each of us has our own story and upbringing, our own unique buttons that push us over the edge, silent gestures that bring us joy, and most of all, we all hold the deep desires of our hearts.

When two unique people come together, it is both a joyous

dance and an uncomfortable act of learning to discover which buttons we must avoid, what gestures we must commit, and how to follow the desires of our hearts without casting aside the responsibilities of our reality.

My dear Zara, I know that you are strong of spirit, and you will demand no less than what you deserve. Of that I have no concern, but I do hope you know that although marriage can be difficult, not everything must be a fight or an uphill battle. I hope that you allow love to be easy. Despite any fear my passing may have brought to you, I hope you know that love is the safest choice to make. And most of all, darling daughter, I hope you know that you are also worthy of the love you are receiving.

I can only imagine that it is a very special man who has stolen your heart. Selfishly, I hope you will tell him about me and that you tell your children how much I would have loved them should you choose to have them. And I pray you always remember the love I have for you.

You are a precious diamond, Zara Bhatta, and it is an honor to see you shine.

Love,

Mom

Tears openly fell down my cheeks, and I held the letter carefully so as not to damage it with my emotion. Ronan reached across the console and held my knee. My silent supporter as always.

Mom had that one right. Ronan was incredible. And we were both accomplishing great things. I only wish that she could have met him. She would have loved his writing, the way he saw the world for all that it is... If only they could have shared a cup of chai together, they would have made fast friends.

I looked up into his dark brown eyes, the ones that were waiting so patiently for me to speak. Over a choked breath, I said, "I wish she could have met you."

"I wish I could have met her too," he said quietly. "I can only imagine how wonderful she was to have earned your love."

"Can I tell you about her?" I asked.

"Of course," he replied.

We stayed in the parking lot for another hour, just talking about my mom and the wonderful woman she was. And as we went back home to make more calls for the fundraiser, I couldn't help but feel a little more whole.

SIXTEEN

RORY

IT WAS the day of our film premiere at the theater, and there was really nothing more that we could do.

My friends and I had walked every square inch of this town, spoken to every business owner, left messages on every number we had, emailed people far and wide, and our fundraising numbers reflected it.

With only $100,000 left to go, I was *really* hoping that between the film and last-minute donations, we would get there. It would be close.

The house was quiet except for "Rory's Song" playing softly through my phone. Beckett had it written for me as a birthday gift. Each lyric touched my heart as I walked to my closet and pulled out a sleek black dress with a slit up the leg. Holding it up, seeing the fabric move and shimmer, brought back so many memories.

I bought this for our first wedding anniversary. We went on a cruise, and this was what I'd worn on the formal night. He'd wore a suit with a dark green shirt that brought out all the colors in his beautiful eyes. In fact, that picture was on our mantel, forever memorializing the love and possibility of early marriage.

That trip was when we'd decided to have a family. When we stopped using birth control and said we would let what happened happen. But after months of "not trying" and nothing happening, I'd taken matters into my own hands.

My fertility trackers stared at me from the bathroom door. I had posted them carefully with double-sided tape, meticulously tracking my basal body temperature to get any hint at when I was ovulating. The red marker so precisely printed on the sheet glared back at me. This was exactly the kind of thing that Beckett didn't like.

He wanted romance. And wasn't that why I fell for him in the first place? He was, after all, the boy who had taken me to the bakery and danced to music playing on his phone when no one was around. He was the boy who'd gotten on his knee in front of a nightclub and given me a cupcake neck-lace to ask me to homecoming. And he was the *man* who knelt before me in front of the big Christmas tree in New York City, asking me to be his wife that Christmas and every Christmas after.

Feeling angry at myself for taking all the romance out of our relationship, I ripped down the charts and crumpled them in my hand before throwing them in our trash can. And what was left behind was an empty door.

I'd expected to feel devastated, lost, after giving up. Instead, I felt free.

Free from the pressure of asking my body to do something it clearly didn't want to do right now.

Free from the guilt of not giving Beckett the child I knew he deserved.

Free from the weight of my infertility and the constant second-guessing that PCOS gave me.

Free from wondering if it was the bagel I had for breakfast or the smoothie for dessert that was causing this rift of infertility in my life and in my marriage.

Free from anything but the future that Beckett and I could have together.

If this fundraiser had shown me anything, it was that I *did* care about other people. I didn't need a child to care for to make a difference in this world and to grow family and to feel love. In fact, hundreds of people had donated to Waldo's Diner in the last two weeks. Hundreds of people had come together to support this mission I cared about. And wasn't that a family all on its own?

It may not have been made of blood, but it was made of love. And I knew if I looked hard enough, I'd see so many people like Chester and Karen. So many causes like Waldo's Diner. And I *would* find joy, if only I opened my eyes to the things that I was lucky enough to have. Friendships that would last a lifetime. Students who looked up to me. A family that cared for me. The love of a good man. Those were the things I should have been tracking on the bathroom door, not everything I lacked.

The bedroom door opened, and I jumped back in surprise, seeing Beckett in his work clothes. "You're home early."

He gave me an easy smile. "Couldn't miss the setup for the big night." He set his camera bag down by the closet, and then his eyes trailed from me to the bathroom door and back again.

An unspoken question rested in the curve of his lips.

Letting out a breath and feeling the sting of

emotion in my eyes, I said two words I usually hated. "You're right."

A gentle smile formed on his lips as he came closer, cupping my face in his calloused hand. I closed my eyes against the gentle brush of his thumb over my cheekbone.

"I've been so proud of you these last two weeks," he said. "It's been like getting my old Aurora back, seeing you stand up for the little guy and putting yourself out there. It's almost like we're in high school again, except I didn't break my wrist and you didn't get covered in cupcakes."

I let out an unexpected laugh. I was so glad we could laugh about that now. "I didn't mean to make our whole lives about my uterus," I said.

He chuckled softly. "You made our lives about our future." He kissed my forehead. "I just wanted to enjoy the present with you."

I wrapped my arms around him and held him. My rock. My love. My life.

As long as I had him, I knew it would all be okay. I knew I had what I needed, and everything else would just be a bonus.

He kissed my lips and then my cheeks, and then he lifted my shirt and kissed my shoulders, the spot over my heart. I let myself get swept away in the moment, in his love.

In our *present*.

Beckett's finger slowly traced up my back as he zipped my black dress. When I turned to him, he covered his mouth and rocked back. "Damn, you're fine."

I laughed out loud. "I could say the same thing about you, Mr. Langley."

"Well, Mrs. Langley," he said, picking up my necklace from the dresser and spinning his finger so I would turn around, "I would say that we'll be the luckiest ones at the theater, but honestly, I'm hoping that'll be Chester and Karen tonight."

I nodded in agreement. "It would be so amazing after everything that they've given to the community for them to see how grateful we are for it. That it hasn't gone unnoticed, you know?"

"Exactly." He clipped the necklace in place and then moved my curls back to cover it. "But, I have to say, I'm excited at the thought of sitting in the back of the movie theater and making out with you tonight."

My cheeks heated. "Beckett!"

He laughed. "Is it my fault I have a smokin' hot wife?"

I rolled my eyes. "You're acting like a teenager."

"That's who you fell in love with, isn't it?" he teased.

I couldn't correct him.

We held hands as we walked out to his car, and he opened the door for me. On the drive across town, we held hands again, and it was like somehow, throwing away those charts had healed us. I felt more in love with him than ever, and I felt more loved than ever.

We reached the theater early, and even though there was regular movie-going traffic in the lobby, we easily spotted the table where some of our friends were already setting up. Ginger and Ray had that calf Oscar on a leash, and Callie and Carson were kneeling, petting it, despite the fact that they were both dressed up. Zara stood at the opposite end of the table, working on the cashbox with Ronan, seemingly getting as far away from the animal as she could.

Jordan and Kai hadn't arrived yet, but I could only hope that they would come together. I knew the future wasn't certain for them, but I hoped with my whole heart that they would figure it out and get the happily ever after they deserved.

Everyone greeted us as we approached the table, and we spent a few minutes fawning over each other and how great we looked. It was almost like going to prom all over again. Except now we had $100,000 to raise and a diner to save.

Soon after we said hello to everyone, Jordan and Kai approached the table. They weren't holding hands like Beckett and I had done, but at least they were together.

Kai said, "We've been getting donations pretty steadily for the last several hours. Hopefully it picks up with the movie purchases."

Callie nodded, getting up and brushing off her knees. "I think some people will probably wait to donate until today when they buy their tickets."

I nodded, hoping she was right.

Someone called hello, and we looked up to see Birdie and her hot silver-fox husband, Cohen, walking toward us with Chester and Karen. They looked like a million bucks, Chester in a charcoal-gray suit with a gold tie and Karen in a beautiful golden dress with three-quarter length sleeves.

We all took turns hugging them, and then Chester stepped back, his eyes already shining.

Clearing his throat, he said, "I can't tell you how much this all means to us. When we worked at the diner, we were happy to give everyone a hot meal when we could and a safe place for kids to hang out on Friday nights. And the fact that you all cared enough about us to put this together..." His voice broke, and he swallowed. "Well, that just means the world to us, whether or not we raise the money."

Tears were already streaming down my cheeks, and I was thankful that I had opted for waterproof mascara.

Callie offered to walk them into the theater and set them in the spot of honor, right in the middle row with the best view, and soon after they went inside, the line began forming. It was longer than I ever imagined and actually went all the way to the back of the parking lot, wrapping around the curb. People from all over had heard about our fundraiser, and they all donated the suggested ticket cost and oftentimes even more.

It was clear, with each dollar spent, just how big of an impact a hot meal and safe place to hang out on Friday night had been.

Callie came back out and said to us, "They're opening up two additional screening rooms to accommodate all these people."

We all cheered together, and I said, "That's amazing, Callie! Thanks for checking on that."

"I thought I had been changing the world as a social worker..." She slowly shook her head. "But it turns out Chester and Karen were the real heroes all along."

THE MANAGER of the movie theater, Fredericka, came to our table and pulled me aside. "Callie, we're closing all of our screening rooms and dedicating them to the documentary."

I glanced at my friends, still busy taking donations. We'd already filled several cash bags, and Beckett was dropping them off at the bank before they closed so we wouldn't have so much cash on hand. The donations were coming in online, through Venmo... It was incredible. But having all of the theater's five screens dedicated to the showing...

"That's amazing," I breathed. "Are you sure?"

She nodded. "There were only a few ticket sales for the other shows, and the people who bought them happily took their refunds so they could catch the movies another time." Fredericka grinned. "I love what you all are doing for Chester and Karen. They're too big a part of this community to let them go."

I agreed. "It's crazy. All this time, I thought it was just a diner."

"It's never that simple, is it?" Fredericka said. "You don't have to do anything fancy to change lives. You just have to provide a service and do it well."

Her words settled on my heart. For years, I'd been working toward a career that people said changed lives... I never even noticed the opportunities that were right in front of me. Maybe I didn't need to worry so much about my next move and simply focus on filling a need.

Fredericka excused herself to help her employees with concessions, and I went back to my friends to tell them the good news.

Ray hugged Ginger and kissed her cheek. "They're going to love your film, babe."

She grinned, her eyes shining in the evening sun. "Chester and Karen deserve to be seen."

Zara nodded happily. "How are we going to manage this? There are five of us couples, so we could each take one theater to announce the film and remind people to donate?"

I nodded. "Who should take Chester and Karen's?"

Everyone looked at me, and Carson put his arm around me. "Honey, you deserve this moment with them."

I was stunned when everyone agreed. I reached out to hold Zara's and Rory's hands, and they linked hands with the other two. "I'm so thankful for you all. It's one thing to have friends in your corner, and it's another to have friends who are changing the world."

We shared a teary-eyed moment, and then it was time. We each went to our theaters, and Carson held my hand as we walked into room one, the one with Chester and Karen in the middle. Without the lights dimmed, we could see them sharing in conversation with each other. The entire room was abuzz with conversation, filled with the community Waldo's Diner had created.

Carson and I went to the front, and he whistled loudly to draw everyone's attention.

I smiled shyly and raised my voice so everyone could hear me.

"My first memory of Waldo's Diner is going

with my mom, dad, and brother for breakfast after church on Sunday. It's where we went to eat, to celebrate, and as I got older, it's where I went with my friends. It's where Carson and I went after dates. And every time I was there, I could count on a smile from Chester." I gestured toward him and his wife. He waved, a proud smile on his face.

"The love he and Karen have for this community is incredible. They've employed people, cared for many, and given kids a safe place to be. The fire that took down the diner was a huge loss, not just to them but for all of us, and all of the funds raised in this campaign are going toward buying the lot and rebuilding the diner so we won't ever have to go without this amazing place."

I smiled at Carson, pride shining in his eyes. "Carson, can you check how much we have left to raise?"

He pulled out his phone and went to the tracker. We'd been updating it as we counted cash and watching to see the online donations came in.

When he held up the screen, my mouth fell open, and I covered it with my hands.

$503,041

"WE'VE REACHED OUR GOAL!" I cried, jumping into Carson's arms.

He held me, spinning me around as cheers broke out around us. "You did it!" he said, setting me down and then holding my face in his hands. He kissed my lips. "You did it, babe."

Tears were falling down my cheeks as the cheers continued around us and in all the other theaters. I looked toward the middle row, seeing Chester and Karen smiling our way, their eyes just as wet as mine.

"Congratulations," I mouthed their way. Chester kissed his wife's hand while she held her free hand to her heart.

As the cheers died down, I said, "Now that we can celebrate, let's watch this movie!"

Carson and I walked toward the back, standing along the wall and watching as the documentary played. Seeing the reactions in everyone, the way people laughed or smiled or even got teary-eyed, it was icing on the cake.

At the end, there was a standing ovation for Chester and Karen. My heart could have burst seeing them get all the attention they deserved.

As everyone filtered out of the theater, Carson and I left, driving to my house, where everyone agreed to meet after the movie. Cori, Ginger's younger sister and our real estate agent, had gotten the seller to agree to wait until tonight for us to submit our offer. So no matter how tonight had gone, we would be deciding our next course of action after this movie.

Carson and I held hands, tired but giddy at the prospect of submitting our final offer, at seeing how happy Chester and Karen would be.

Carson parked along the curb so there would be room in the driveway, and we went inside. Mom had snack trays ready, so I got them out of the refrigerator and set them at the kitchen table so we could have some snacks after such a long day.

Being able to support my friends this way, with such a small gesture, felt good. Maybe I had a little more of Chester and Karen's spirit in me than I ever realized.

A knock on the door sounded before Cori and her fiancé, Ryker, came inside. They looked like a million bucks, as always. She came and gave me a hug, a huge smile on her face. "I can't believe we get to submit this offer!"

"I know!" I said in agreement. I wasn't waxing eloquent tonight, because my feelings were all over the place. After the tumult of the last couple weeks, I couldn't wait to have our offer in and accepted. To seal the deal on saving Waldo's Diner.

My parents came in next, congratulating us before going back to their room to get ready for bed. And soon we were all there...

All of us except for Chester and Karen.

I tried calling them but got no answer. Again.

"Where are they?" I asked my friends. "Have they called any of you?"

They all shook their heads. I checked my phone again, seeing it had been an hour and a half since the movie had ended. "Do you think we should call the police?" I asked. "Could they have been in an accident?"

Concern was clear on my friends' faces, but Jordan said, "Let's give them another half hour before we start worrying too much..."

That didn't stop me from searching *car accidents in Emerson, California.*

But then the doorbell rang, and I hurried to the door, pulling it open. Chester and Karen were there, thankfully in one piece.

"Come in!" I said. "We were so worried about you! Did you have a hard time finding the house?"

Chester and Karen exchanged a look, and even though they both appeared to be healthy, my stomach sank. This was not good news.

Karen nodded at Chester, and he took a heavy breath.

"I can't thank you kids enough for all that you've done for us," he began, sincerity clear in each of his features. "Someone sits long enough in a diner, watching life around them, and they wonder if they're making a difference. What you have done for Karen and me…" He squeezed her hand. "It's the best gift we've ever received. But we have to be honest with you. Before the diner burned down, we'd been talking about retiring, maybe letting go of the business and having the landlord lease to someone else. We're getting older, and running a business like that ain't easy. After hearing how excited you all were about the project, we thought maybe we could hang on to it for a little while longer, but we just don't have the energy we used to. We can't, in good conscience, let you use all these donations to support a business that might not be here in a few years."

With each word he spoke, I felt my heart breaking a little more. No more Waldo's Diner. No matter how hard we'd fought to save it, we couldn't make him run it.

Rory was the first to speak, saying, "We sure are going to miss seeing you at the diner, Chester."

He extended his hand, his voice raw as he said, "My door's always open, kid."

She went and hugged him, then we all took our turns until Chester and Karen said it was time for them to get home.

And despite the fact that all my friends were in the house after they left, my heart felt empty. Once again, I'd lost a dream... and I didn't know what could possibly come next.

EIGHTEEN

JORDAN

THERE WERE twelve of us sitting around Callie's living room, trying to process the highs and lows of everything that had just happened. Tears were streaming down Callie's cheeks as she held on to Carson. Rory leaned against Beckett's shoulder, and Ginger and Ray solemnly held each other's hands. Even Cori and Ryker had their feet crossing. Kai and I were barely touching each other.

And I knew it was a crappy way to feel, but honestly, I was pissed. These last two weeks, I'd spent every spare minute on fundraising when I should have been saving my relationship. If Chester and Karen showed me something tonight, it was that I needed to be true to myself, even if it made others uncomfortable.

My mom was moving on, getting married, all while I'd neglected my own relationship. Kai had been there for me through so much, even when it meant going against his dad and the traditional path. He'd helped me understand that money wasn't bad. It was a tool. And just like any other tool, it could be wielded for good or evil.

He'd shown me that I deserved a love that lasted.

He'd spent hours, days, weeks looking for the precious necklace my mother pawned.

And he'd stood by my side through my under-grad degree, through my first two years of med school and clinical rotations.

All he asked was that I dedicated time to our relationship. To him.

And I'd lost track of what really mattered.

Chester and Karen had been brave to be true to us about what they wanted. And now it was time for me to start being true to Kai. He was my family, and I *couldn't* lose him.

I stood up, reaching for his hand. "Let's go home."

My friends looked at us, and Zara said, "Aren't you going to stay and help us figure this out?"

Shaking my head, I said, "We did all we could for them. It's up to them to decide if they want the help or not."

Kai added, "We can start refunding donations from the website next week. I just want a weekend to spend with my girl."

Despite all the disappointment, my heart warmed. I was still his girl. I weaved my fingers through his, and we walked out of Callie's house toward his car parked out front. It wasn't the dented Honda he'd traded his car in for in high school. Turns out, when you buy cheap cars, you pay in repairs. Now he drove a much less flashy Buick sedan with a sleek black exterior and tan leather seats that were easy to wipe down.

He held the door open for me, and I thanked him before getting in. His black eyes glittered in the streetlight glow as he briefly smiled down at me. He leaned in and pressed a swift kiss to my lips, then walked to his side of the car.

My heart fluttered as I watched him in his suit. This was my person, and I needed to make it work.

When he got in, I extended my hand, palm up. He glanced my way as he slipped his fingers through mine.

"I'm proud of you," he said.

I raised my eyebrows, because I was pretty sure all my friends were upset with me for what I said.

"I am." He squeezed my hand. "Do you remember high school, Jordan? You would have been so floored that someone could refuse help. That all that money was looking them in the face and they walked away. You've grown so much, and I am; I'm proud as hell of who you've become."

He put the car in drive and pulled away from Callie's house while my smile slowly grew.

He was right.

Back in high school, I was on a mission to "save" people like my mom and me, but some people didn't want to be rescued. I understood that now.

Chester and Karen had all they needed in each other and the legacy they had left.

"Can we talk about us?" I asked.

He looked over at me and asked, "Should I pull over?" What he was really asking was, *Is this bad news?*

"No," I said. "Unless you want to."

He slowed the car anyway and parked along a curb in a residential area. All the homes and yards were quiet, mostly devoid of light except for a soft orange glow coming through a few windows.

With the car parked, he unbuckled and turned toward me. I did the same, then linked our hands once again. I looked in his eyes, remembering the gaze that always captivated me. Trailed my eyes down his arms, so strong and capable of protecting or comforting me.

"Kai, I know I've been less than a stellar partner for you with my clinicals and my mom's engagement. It's been all-consuming, and I took the fact that you'd be there for me for granted."

His throat moved as he swallowed, and his eyes filled with moisture before he looked away, still holding on to my hand. "I thought you didn't care about me anymore," he said, his voice thick with emotion.

His admission broke my heart. I reached out, taking his face in both my hands. "You're not just my boyfriend, Kai. You're my *family*." My voice broke on the last word, and he reached out, holding on to my hands on his cheeks. "I know you want us to go to therapy, and I'm sure we need it, but I don't want to figure out if we're going to make it work. I want to see how therapy can make *us* stronger."

"I'd love that," he breathed, blinking a tear down his cheek.

I leaned closer and kissed him, and I didn't know which tears were his or mine. "Kai, I want to be with you forever. I want to be your wife. I want to have your kids. I want to sit with you on the front porch in rockers with peeling paint from overuse. Most of all, I just want to be by your side."

"Will you marry me?" he asked.

The question shocked me. We'd always talked about someday, after college. After I had a job. After we were established. But all that was doing was signaling to Kai that he came after all my dreams.

"Yes," I said. "Yes!"

There was no ring. No kneeling on one knee in front of a sunset beach. But it was him and me, and that was all that mattered.

He hugged me close across the console, then kissed me and kissed me and kissed me. And even though we were in a residential area, I climbed to his side of the car and loved him the way he deserved to be loved.

With our cheeks red and my hair a mess, we rode away from our parking spot. When we stopped at a stop sign, I stared at the street name.

"Kai," I breathed, pointing.

He looked at the sign and read it out loud. "Juana St."

It was a sign. From my sister. From the universe, that we were exactly where we were meant to be.

RYKER and I walked out to his truck, and I got in, feeling completely helpless. I'd been going over this deal for the last two weeks, pulled every string I had to get the agent to agree to wait until my sister and her friends could raise the money, and now... it was all slipping through their fingers.

Callie especially had been devastated.

And letting the deal go... it just didn't feel right.

Ryker started the pickup, then reached over and rubbed my knee. "I'm sorry, babe. I know you worked hard on this."

"It's not just that," I said to him and myself... "I feel like I'm letting them down, like this deal was meant to go through."

He studied me with his gray eyes. "Then submit it."

"Submit it?" I asked.

"You have their paperwork, don't you? You can submit it, and then you have fourteen days for the inspection period. You can buy them a little more time. Two weeks could change everything."

"It's crazy," I replied. "I know it is, but my gut..."

"Your gut is never wrong." He lifted my hand and kissed my knuckles. "So be the Cori I know you are and submit the deal. I'll be waiting for the magic to happen."

RAY and I got in the truck and started driving toward home. At least, I thought that's where we were going. "Ray, you missed our turn."

"I didn't," he said, continuing down the road.

I pointed behind us. "That was the exit for the highway."

"We're not going that way."

My eyebrows drew together. "Then where are we going?"

"Your mom and dad said we could stay there tonight. I thought it was a good idea."

Okay, now I was frustrated. "We're staying at my parents'? And you didn't even warn me?"

"If I warned you, would you have gone?"

"No."

He gave me a look like that was exactly the point.

"Ray, you can't force me to make up with my parents."

"No, but I can force you to be in the room with them long enough to talk it out or kill each other."

I glared at him, knowing his stubborn streak ran just as deep as mine. He wasn't backing down. So I had to try a different tactic.

"Ray, it's been a long day. I'm tired. I just want to go home and go to bed. We can talk to my parents next weekend. I promise."

He laughed out loud.

"What!"

"You're the worst liar." He turned into my family's neighborhood and parked along a side street. I recognized the Tudor-style house next to us. I'd driven by it every day on my way into school. And even though it had a fresh coat of paint now, it was still the same.

"I don't want to be back here," I said.

"They're your family," he replied.

"And? That automatically excuses their bad behavior?"

"No, but it means you'll put up with it long enough for them to say they're sorry."

"My mom won't."

He let out a sigh. "Ginger, you've got to give her a chance!"

"That's up to me," I argued. "I know you want us all to be one big happy family, but life doesn't work that way."

Ray looked out the window for a moment and then finally met my eyes again.

"Don't do it," I said.

"Damn it, I'm doing it." He gripped the steering wheel tightly. "I lost my dad when I was fourteen years old, Ginger. That's ten years of going without him for birthdays, for farm work, for our wedding, and someday, without him seeing his grandchildren. And it wasn't like he was sick and I knew it was coming. He just died, Ging. One day there, the next day gone. And life is too damn short for you not to work this out with your parents. I'm thankful as hell that you don't understand why you can't let this go on, but you have to make things right with them. If not for yourself, for me."

My eyes stung with tears at his loss, for what I had been missing out on. Because if I was being honest, I wanted the kind of friendship with my mom that Jordan shared with hers. I wanted to invite her over to dinners on the farm and not worry about her asking what kind of ingredients I included. If it was all organic. I wanted them to be able to watch our future children and trust my judgment.

I wanted them to be proud of me.

"What if they never change?" I asked, my voice breaking. "What if they always see me as an incompetent child?"

He smiled with one side of his mouth. "Then we love them as best we can, even though they don't know the truth like we do."

"And what is the truth?" I asked.

He reached across, holding my face in his hand and brushing his thumb across my cheek. "The truth is that you are a loyal friend, an incredible wife, a skilled entrepreneur, and capable of achieving whatever you set your mind to."

I held on to his hand, on to his truth, and nodded. "I'll do this for you," I said. Although, the truth was... I needed it for me too.

I sat back in my seat and nodded, and he drove the rest of the way to my childhood home. The white bungalow stared back at me, with its green lawn and the Ripe sign posted by the driveway. There were the garden gnomes and a light shining in the living room window.

We got out of the truck, and Ray reached into the toolbox in the truck bed, pulling out a duffel bag he'd packed for us.

"You're sneaky," I said, nodding toward the bag.

He put his arm around me. "I love you."

"Yeah, yeah, love you too."

We walked to the front door, and he pressed the bell. It rang a few times before the door swung open. My mom and dad stood in the doorway, Dad in shorts and a T-shirt, Mom in her nighttime robe.

"Come in, come in," Mom said.

Ray gave her a hug, then shook my dad's hand. "Thanks for having us. It was a late night at the theater."

I followed Ray in and accepted an awkward hug from Mom.

Dad cleared his throat. "We'll let you two get to bed. Ginger, your room's made up. The twins are at a sleepover with a friend, so don't worry about being quiet on your way back there."

Thankful for the exit, I walked down the familiar hallway to the room I used to share with Cori. As soon as I stepped inside and flicked on the light, I realized just how different it was.

Both of our twin beds were gone now, replaced instead with a king-sized bed in the middle of the room, trendy wire nightstands on each side. Hanging lamps had been strung from the ceiling, and they glowed on each side of the bed.

In fact, it looked like neither Cori nor I had ever been here. And even though I'd taken everything important to me, it felt strange that the space was so different.

"They redecorated," I said to Ray.

He set our bag down on the end of the bed. "Maybe they were looking for a fresh start."

I nodded quietly and waited for him to unzip the bag, pulling out some of my silk pajamas and my asthma inhaler. I took a couple of puffs, then brought my pajamas with me to my old bathroom. This had been redecorated too with new tile and a completely new vanity. It was beautiful. And part of me wondered why change the place now. Had Mom been looking for things to occupy her time with Cori and me out of the house?

Of course, the supplies in the bathroom were no different. Paraben- and sulfate-free cleansers rested on the sink. In the drawer, I saw a supply of mineral makeup for the twins—the same kind Cori and I had been allowed to use. And through the new glass shower doors, I saw the same shampoo and conditioner, right down to the rosemary mint scent.

Some things never changed.

I washed my face and then dressed in my pajamas, going back to the bedroom where Ray was already lying under the covers.

"You look right at home," I said.

He glanced around the room. "The teenage boy in me is pumped I'm sleeping over in my girlfriend's room." He kissed me deeply.

I drew back, grinning. "I'm your wife now. Nowhere near as exciting."

"No way. We could be eighty years old with gray hair and wrinkles, and I'd still be excited to lie down next to you."

My heart fluttered. "Have I mentioned how lucky I am to have you?"

"Doesn't hurt to hear it again," he said, opening his arm so I could lie on his shoulder.

After a few minutes of resting together, his breathing steadied and slowed until I glanced over and saw him asleep. His dark brown eyelashes fanned against his cheeks, and his full lips were slightly parted.

He was beautiful. And my heart swelled at how

much he loved me. How much he supported my family.

But the thought of talking to my mom tomorrow, it had me on edge. I didn't want to fight. I just wanted to live my life. But I knew if we were to move forward, I'd have to stand my ground and find a compromise with my parents.

I glanced at the clock—past midnight, but my stomach was growling. I rolled out of bed and made my way to the kitchen, wondering if there was still a stash of chocolate chips in the cabinet.

I didn't have a chance to find out, though, because when I reached the kitchen, I found my mom leaning against the island, drinking a mug of tea with a photo album spread in front of her.

"I'm sorry," I said. "I didn't mean to interrupt."

"It's okay," she replied. "There's a stash of snacks you might like in the far cabinet."

So I'd been right... I retrieved some chocolate chips and poured myself a glass of water, fully intending to go back to bed. Until Mom said, "Sometimes I forget how little you all were. You were ten when the twins were born, but you look so much younger here."

I glanced at the photo album, seeing Cori and me sitting on the couch, a newborn twin in each of our laps. That was a few years before my asthma got bad. I looked so proud holding one twin. So carefree.

"I forgot how bald they were," I said. You could barely see little wisps of red hair against their pale skin.

Mom turned the page, showing the twins just a few months later. "They didn't get hair until they were fourteen months old. We thought they'd be bald forever." She laughed.

I watched her for a moment, lost in memory lane.

"The bedroom looks good," I said.

"The bedroom?" She looked at me like I'd yanked her from the past. "Oh. We wanted to make sure you had a comfy place to stay if you ever..."

"Came back?" I finished.

She lifted her eyebrows, flipping the page again. "I look through these pictures, and I think, if I would have known back then that you'd hate me so much..." Her voice broke.

I froze, holding on tightly to my bowl and glass. "Mom, I don't hate you."

"What is it then?" She met my eyes, and for the first time, I realized she'd been crying. "What did I do so wrong?"

I glanced toward the hallway, my exit route, and then back to my mom, shrinking in front of me. She was hurting—I could tell—but I was hurting too.

"Do you really want to get into this now?" I asked. The digital clock above the cabinets said it was well past one.

"Please," she whispered.

"Mom, I've been out of the house for six years, married for two, and you still treat me like a child! After high school, I thought you were starting to trust me more, but you can't even come over to my house without throwing away a cleaning supply or making a comment about the food in my refrigerator. And how's this supposed to work when the baby gets here? I'm supposed to feel incompetent to take care of myself but have a child depending on me?"

Her eyes were wide. "Baby? Are you..."

My cheeks heated instantly. "We're... trying. And, Mom, I'm scared as hell. I want to feel like I can do this, but I never feel good enough in your eyes."

"Oh, honey..." Her hand went to her parted lips. "I never knew that's how I was making you feel. I always thought I was just... taking care of you."

"Mom, I'm twenty-five years old. I need a friend more than I need a parent."

She nodded slowly. "I promise I'll back off. But will you please let me back in your life?"

I studied her carefully. "No more judgmental comments about my food?"

"None."

"No more swapping my cleaning supplies for ones you like?"

"Cross my heart."

"No more double-checking that I'm keeping my appointments and taking my treatments?"

"Babe, I'm just trying to—"

"No, Mom. If this is going to work, if I'm going to be a mom, I need to be in charge of myself. I'll come to you for help, always, when I need it and want it. But can you just... be proud of me for who I am?"

Tears fell down her cheeks. "Of course, Ginger. I love you, always, and I am so proud of the life and career you've created. It was never what I imagined for you, but somehow it's so much better."

My own throat felt tight at her admission. I knew people had thought I should be working in the city, in Hollywood, but my life... I loved it and the fact that my mom loved it too.

I went and hugged her tight. "I'm sorry," I said, crying too. "I shouldn't have held such a grudge against you... I just didn't want to be ashamed anymore."

She held my face in her hands, brushing back my hair. "You never need to be ashamed around me." She kissed my forehead. "I love you, Ginger. That will never change." Then she said something that healed all the broken parts of my heart I never knew existed.

"You're going to be an amazing mom."

TWENTY-ONE
ZARA

SUNDAY NIGHT, Ronan and I lay on the couch. I had on my favorite black silk pajamas, and he made a mug of chai for me just like my mom used to. I sipped the hot, spicy liquid, trying not to feel disappointed in how everything had gone down. Or in the fact that Ronan and I would never get to have our wedding reception at Waldo's Diner.

He took my foot resting in his lap and rubbed it in his hands. "What do you think of India?"

I gave him an amused look. "The country?"

He closed his eyes, shaking his head. "For our wedding."

That took my mind off the disappointment. "You want to get married in India?"

"I was thinking... I don't have any family here,

and most of your dad's side of the family is still in India. He and your mom got married there. It might be a way for you to feel connected to her."

He looked up from my foot to me with those dark eyes, so much emotion swirling beneath the surface.

"You would do that?" I whispered.

He nodded.

"You'd travel around the world, go through a big Indian wedding, and ride in on a white horse... for me."

He gripped my hand and pulled me closer so he could kiss me. "Hold on."

Sliding from under my leg, he got up and jogged to his desk, scribbling on a piece of paper. Writing words and crossing them out.

When he came back, he said, "I think I have my vows."

I looked at the piece of paper, reading the words he'd written. "I promise to cross all the oceans for you. Ride every wave. Dance through the highest flames. Because in your heart is where mine tames."

My lips parted. "Did you really just write that?"

He nodded, kneeling in front of me and twining his fingers through mine. "Zara, I've always known you were home. Wherever we choose to celebrate our love is less important than the person I'm celebrating with."

Tears burned in my eyes as I pulled him close and kissed him.

"You're crying," he whispered, using his thumbs to wipe them away.

"I'm happy," I said. "And my dad's going to be crying too when he finds out he's going to be able to plan a big Indian wedding. And the business has enough points; I'm sure we can fly our friends there. It's going to be incredible."

His smile melted my heart. "I'm happy you're happy."

I DROVE INTO SCHOOL, completely exhausted since my spring break hadn't been much of a vacation. As soon as I got inside, I went to the teachers' lounge pouring myself a giant mug of coffee.

"Hey, you," Birdie said from behind me.

I turned to see her holding a ceramic mug Carson's sister Sierra had made Birdie in art class. It made me smile to know she still used it. "Oh, hey," I said, replacing the coffee pot.

She gave me a knowing smile. "Long week, huh?"

I nodded, leaning back against the counter to drink my coffee. "I think the hardest part of it was seeing Callie's face afterward. She cried for hours that night, and Carson eventually just had us go home."

Sympathy flooded Birdie's features. "Callie's always had such a big heart."

I nodded. "It's not just that. I think she felt like she was really succeeding at something for the first time in years."

"Do you think she could work in fundraising with her dad?"

"I don't think it was the fundraising," I said. "Just the cause. She really felt like the diner was changing lives by providing a safe space for so many kids. I mean, we all did."

Birdie nodded, patting my shoulder. "Sometimes life's biggest disappointments are also our biggest learning moments. This might set Callie on a better path, even if it doesn't look how she hoped it would."

I nodded, wondering if that's what infertility was doing for Beckett and me. If it had given us lessons we would use whether or not we became parents.

Birdie filled her mug, and we walked together down the quiet hallway as students slowly began filtering into the school.

"Hey," Birdie said, "I heard Anna was bringing

back some gourds from Arizona for art class?"

My smile widened. It had been six years since I tutored Anna, and having her in my class now was such a joy. "We're going to make birdhouses for the students to set out this spring. I'm *so* excited."

"That sounds like a blast," Birdie said. "If you have an extra, I'd love to hang it in my office. Ralphie wouldn't fit, but I think he'd like the extra decoration in his cage."

"Anything for Ralphie," I said with a grin. That bird was as much a part of this school as the Latin inscriptions above the door.

We reached her door, and she paused with her hand on the knob. "Rory? I know it's a Monday morning, but do you mind if I say something sentimental?"

I couldn't help but laugh. "I think sentimentality is what keeps me going these days."

She covered her mug with her other hand. "All those years ago, when I heard from Mr. Davis what you girls were plotting in the A/V room, I have to admit, I was a little nervous that it was only a way to get back at Merritt. But the more I saw you girls and watched your friendship bloom, the more I knew you had something so incredibly special. You five were always looking for ways to give the little people a voice, whether it was girls who were picked on or guys who were overlooked... or an older man who sat in a diner booth. There have been six versions of the 'curvy girl club' so far, and I have to say, you five, the OGs..." She glanced down at her cup smiling. "I'm so proud of the women you've become."

Unable to hold back my emotion, I hugged her with moisture streaming down my cheeks.

"I love you, Birdie B," I said into her shoulder.

"Love you too, sweetie pea."

She gave me a final pat on the back before I walked down the hallway to the room where I spent most of my days, surrounded by students just like me—doing the best they could with what they had.

I sat at my desk, ready to greet the first period learning and rolled my mug in my hands. Anna had made me this mug, spattered a million different colors for our day that we'd learned spelling with the chalk.

I remembered the words I'd spoken that day and held them close to my heart... Sometimes beautiful things are broken.

Maybe it was okay that our dream of rebuilding Waldo's Diner was broken. I just couldn't see the art through the pieces. Yet.

TWENTY-THREE
CARSON

CALLIE HAD SLEPT most of the day on Saturday, and it took all my convincing powers to get her to come out to eat with me for breakfast on Sunday.

We pulled up to the Seaton Bakery parking lot. The daily special may have gone up by fifty cents since we graduated high school, and the gravel parking lot had gotten a couple extra loads of dirt, but it looked exactly the same.

As we got out, Callie said, "It's too bad Gayle and Chris are on that Alaskan cruise. I wish I could say hi to them."

I put my arm around her. "We'll have plenty of time to come by and hang out when we're back for good."

She smiled up at me. "I am excited to be coming home."

The lift in her mood instantly made me feel lighter. "Have you looked at any apartments online yet? Or maybe even a house?"

She shook her head. We paused talking to order some breakfast at the counter and then went to sit down with our coffees in hand.

"You're thinking we should renta a house?" she asked.

I nodded. "Or buy. There's this program for first-time homebuyers where you only have to put down three and a half percent for the loan. I think it could be a really good way for us to get started here. And your parents have been hinting at me that they're really excited to help us move back. Maybe they'd chip in some or let us stay with them while we save."

Callie rolled her eyes. "They're just hoping they have a grandbaby soon."

I winked. "I'm hoping we can practice making grandbabies soon."

She laughed and gave me an admonishing smile. "You're a child."

"Sometimes," I agreed. "But you'll be happy to know I can do adulty things from time to time."

She raised her eyebrows. "Let's hear about them."

"I started looking at jobs, and I found a few openings at rec centers in Emerson and Brentwood..." I paused, still in disbelief about this option. "I even saw that there's an opening for a gym teacher at the Academy's elementary school."

Callie's mouth fell open in a stunned grin. "Carson! You'd be so good at that! All of your nieces and nephews love you, and you can make that program so much fun. Plus you'd get to work with Rory and Birdie!"

I nodded. I'd been hesitant to look at a teaching job because my childhood had been so hard, but it wasn't the school that had hurt me. In fact, schools always gave me a safe place away from my parents. Some adults there even cared enough about me to support me and give me a chance to shine athletically. If I could give that to another kid while I was there, that would mean a lot to me.

"Have you applied?" she asked.

"Last night."

"That's awesome! I could enjoy the whole summer with you, and then we can both go back to work in the fall."

I loved that she was making plans for the future

again. When she was working in the foster care system, it felt like we were just surviving each day. I wanted more of this hope for her. "What are you thinking about doing?"

She frowned. "Honestly?"

I nodded.

"I was hoping we could rebuild Waldo's Diner so I could get a job waiting tables there. Maybe spend some more time around Chester and Karen and figure out how I can do what they're doing."

I took a sip of my coffee. "You know what they're doing, Cal."

"What do you mean?" she asked.

"They have a restaurant." I laughed. Sometimes this girl couldn't see what was right in front of her. This was simple. "They smile at everyone who comes through the door. They serve really great food, treat their workers well. I don't see why you couldn't do exactly that."

"Well, next time I have enough money to buy a restaurant, I will definitely consider that option," she said sarcastically.

But then it hit me. We *did* have enough money to buy a restaurant.

"What?" Callie asked.

"Nothing," I said. I didn't want to get her hopes

up for something I didn't even know was possible yet. And luckily, our food came, so we were occupied by that for the next half hour.

When we got back to her parents' house, I said, "Why don't you go in? I want to drive by the Academy. For old time's sake."

Callie smiled at me and put her hand on my cheek. "They'd be crazy to turn you down."

"I love you," I said, covering her hand with mine.

"I love you too."

I watched her walk to the front door—because damn, my girl looked fine walking away. She gave me a little wave at the door, and then I drove away from the house. After getting a few blocks away, I parked, going through my phone for Cori's number. Once I located it, I hit dial and held it to my ear.

"Hey, Carson, what's up?" she said. I could hear the background noise in her car like she had me on Bluetooth.

"I just had a quick question."

"Shoot."

I bit my lip. "*Hypothetically*, would it even be possible to still buy Waldo's Diner if Chester and Karen change their mind?"

She was quiet for a moment. "This is all hypo-thetical?"

"Sure."

"*Hypothetically*, I haven't told anyone the deal's canceled yet because I'm hoping and praying someone changes their mind."

I laughed and shook my head. "I like you, Cori."

"Back at you," she said. "Let me know if something happens, and we can keep this deal alive."

"I will," I agreed.

I put my phone in the console and pulled away from the curb, driving toward Chester and Karen's home. When Callie visited them, she had gone on and on about how cute the neighborhood was and how she wanted a house that looked like theirs someday. So when I arrived, their home was unmistakable.

Plus, Chester and Karen were sitting on their front porch, a pitcher of what looked like tea between them, books in both of their hands. They were enjoying their retirement. I just hoped they'd be open to helping me out.

As I pulled along the street, they looked my way. As I got out of the car and they recognized me, they smiled.

"Carson?" Chester said. "What brings you here?"

"I wanted to talk to you. I have an idea."

TWENTY-FOUR
CALLIE

MOM AND DAD were out with their friends, playing a round of early afternoon golf, so I sat at the kitchen table with my computer, scrolling through job listings and trying to find one that sounded as good as working with Chester and Karen at Waldo's Diner. There was an opening for a server at La Belle, but it wasn't the same. I called Seaton Bakery, praying Gayle and Chris would have a full-time opening, but the employee there said they only needed a couple part-time workers to help with baking and on the weekends, so that was a bust.

I even looked at jobs my education would qualify me for, but after my experience at my first job, the thought of working as a social worker again made my skin crawl. Part of me wished I could just go back to volunteering at the animal shelter. But I needed to make money. Carson and I had goals to reach, a home to buy, before we settled down with a family.

The front door opened, and I turned to see Carson coming inside.

"Hey, babe," I said, resting my chin in my hand.

"I need to talk to you about something," he said.

The eagerness in his voice had me sitting up. "What's going on?"

He slid into a chair across from me and closed my computer. "It could be big, babe."

My heart started beating quickly, from fear or excitement, I didn't know. "Did you get the job already?"

He shook his head. "It's not that. I just went to talk to Chester and Karen."

"Did they change their mind?" I asked, already excited.

"Not exactly."

I slumped. "What is it?"

He reached across the table, taking my hand. "I

talked to them about how much you admired them and how you wanted to do something similar with your life but didn't have the money to buy a restaurant and didn't really know anyone who was doing something similar."

I bit my lip, hoping good news would follow.

"Chester said even though he didn't want to open the restaurant himself, he'd be willing to spend a year training someone on how to run it and do a rent-to-own agreement on the building."

My jaw dropped. "What?"

Carson nodded, an excited smile on his face. "He said he could teach you everything he knows about making the diner work and keeping the staff happy, and at the end of the year, he would bow out. You'd rent the building from them until your rent made enough to pay it off—at a very low price. He wouldn't accept anything close to market value because of the fundraising situation."

I shook my head, still not believing it. "What about the people who were working there before? Won't they be jealous? I don't want to step on any toes."

"Chester said before the place burned down, he'd been putting out feelers among his staff. Even

Betty wasn't interested in buying the place, said she had too much going on with her new husband. Apparently, his mom is just as sick as hers was."

"Ugh, poor Betty can't catch a break."

Carson nodded.

"And what about my friends? Won't they be upset that they did this for Chester and then all of a sudden I'm cashing in on it?"

"We can talk to your friends about it, but the community will be happy that Waldo's is here to stay. You saw how everyone supported them; heck, you helped film that documentary! This place is important to them. Someone should see it through."

I looked at the table, my mind spinning. Could this be real?

Carson took both of my hands in his. "Callie, this could be the opportunity you were looking for. A chance to change the world and serve people the way you like to do—it just looks different than we thought it would when we were eighteen."

Moisture was already pooling in my eyes. "Are you sure about this? Running a diner is a lot of work. A lot of long nights."

"It is," he agreed. "But you have four best

friends who would do anything for you. A husband who loves you. Parents and a brother who support you like crazy. I really think you can do this. But only if you want to."

That, I still had to decide.

I WAS WALKING out of the dress shop with my bridesmaids' gown when I got a call from Carson.

I drew my eyebrows together and answered. I don't think I'd ever gotten a call from him before except to surprise Callie one year with a visit to North Carolina. "Carson? Is everything okay?"

"It is. I'm trying to get everyone together before I have to head out of town. Are you free tonight?"

"Tonight?" I asked. "Kai and I were planning on going on a date..."

"Can you both come before your date? Please? It's time sensitive."

I popped the trunk of my car to put my dress inside. "What time?"

"Six?"

"We'll be there."

After putting my dress in the car, I walked back to the sidewalk. There was a jewelry shop nearby I wanted to check out. I walked to the end of the block until I stood at the door to Memories jewelry store. The same place that had made Juana's necklace.

Back when Juana was diagnosed with cancer, one of Mom's friends had gotten Juana a necklace. Even though she was only three when she got sick, she'd always felt like a princess with her special necklace. And now that Juana was gone, Mom wore it every single day.

I pushed through the door, making a bell clang overhead, and a saleswoman in a black dress greeted me. "Hi, is there anything I can help you with?"

I nodded, looking around at all the glass cases filled with rings and pendants and bracelets. "I'm looking for a necklace for my mom. She's getting married next weekend."

"We have a great selection of pendants right over here." She walked me to the corner of the store, and we stood before a case filled with different necklace charms. There was everything from animal shapes to birthstones and more.

I studied them, wondering what Mom might love as much as she loved the one she wore. Then my eyes landed on the perfect one. "Can I have that?"

She smiled at me. "That's my favorite. Let me ring it up for you."

Kai and I drove to Callie's house together, dressed for our date. We were going to the Emerson Museum of Modern Art and then out to dinner at La Belle, so our clothes were a little fancier than my usual scrubs and white lab coat. In fact, I felt beautiful in this flowy purple dress and heels with clear straps. I'd even taken a few minutes to paint my toenails and fingers a pretty shade of plumb.

As we pulled up, I noticed all of our friends' vehicles lining the street.

Kai parked behind Beckett's car and said, "Wonder what Carson wanted everyone here for. Do you think they're announcing a pregnancy?"

"I don't think so... Callie just left her job, and

he's getting ready to move here in a couple weeks—I don't see them trying for a baby right now."

"I mean, not all babies come on purpose," he pointed out as he shut off the car.

"True." I got out of the vehicle and walked toward him, linking our fingers together. Kai and I have had a few pregnancy scares over the last several years of our relationship, but only one had resulted in a baby.

I'd never forget seeing the pregnancy test turn pink—the fear I felt for taking care of another human mingled with the excitement of knowing I'd have a child part Kai and part me. Someone to love and protect fiercely with my best friend.

But at our first sonogram appointment, the doctor came in with a sad look in his eyes, telling me the pregnancy had failed. He'd said it like that. Not "your baby has died." Which was what had happened.

I'd cried for months. Throwing myself into my studies was the only thing that had saved me. But now I realized I had left Kai alone with his grief. Was that when the rift had started?

We reached the last step, and I glanced over at him, holding back tears.

"What?" he asked.

I shook my head, blinking. "I just love you is all."

He smiled gently. "I love you too." He gave my hand another squeeze before ringing the doorbell. Time to figure out what this last-minute meeting was all about.

I NUZZLED Oscar's long face, smiling all the while. He was doing so amazing and had so much more energy than he had the day we rescued him. Bottle-feeding him in the morning and evening had quickly become one of my favorite chores around the farm.

"If you don't get going, you're going to be late," Ray called.

I looked away from Oscar to see Ray leaning against the fence panel. His arms hung over the top and his boot rested on the bottom rung and... "Have I told you how sexy you look when you do that?"

He gave me a sun-soaked grin. "Why do you think I keep doing it?"

Oscar bumped against my hip, leaving a slobbery spot on my jeans.

"I haven't forgotten you," I said, rubbing his neck and behind his ears. Then I walked to the gate. Ray held it open for me, then shut it, giving Oscar a pet through the panel.

"Are you sure it's okay that I stay here?" he asked. "I could probably ask Colton to fill in."

"It's no biggie," I said, giving him a kiss on the cheek. At the end of the day, his skin was always a little rougher, and I loved the texture under my lips. My eyes watered. I loved everything about this man, this life.

His face pinched with concern, and he brushed his hand along my cheek. "Are you okay, babe?"

I nodded, sniffing back more moisture. "Happy tears. I swear, I'm so emotional lately."

"Lately?" he teased.

I shoved him playfully.

Chuckling, he put his arm around my shoulders and walked me to my car. "I'll see you when you get back. Drive safe, okay? There are—"

"Deer out at night, I know, I know," I said.

"Can't blame me for worrying."

"I can't." I kissed his lips.

He slapped my butt. "Get out of here."

"Okay, okay," I laughed. And I swear, I smiled all the way to Callie's house. I'd spent so long on my goodbye with Ray that there were already cars lining the street. As I parked and got out of the car, I wondered what their neighbors thought. If they'd hoped for a little less traffic after Callie got out of high school.

Joke's on them, especially now that we'd all reconnected so well.

When I got to the front door, Callie's mom answered with a warm smile. "Hi, Ging, the gang's all downstairs."

"Thanks," I replied with a smile and headed that way. Everyone else was already there. Jordan and Kai were dressed up, Zara and Ronan looked as edgy and fabulous as ever. Rory and Beckett sat side by side, holding hands, and Callie and Carson sat on the coffee table in front of everyone. Even Cori and Ryker were there.

"Hey," I said to the group, giving Cori a side hug. "I didn't know you'd be here."

She gave me a grin I knew by heart. She was keeping a secret.

"What's going on?" I asked no one in particular.

Carson said, "That's why we asked you here."

He looked to Callie, who wore a nervous smile on her face. "Go ahead, babe."

I slid onto the couch between Ryker and Beckett, waiting for her to speak.

She took a breath. "You all know that Carson and I are moving back to Emerson permanently. But since I don't want to do social work anymore, I've been looking for a job. I've been so inspired by Chester and Karen, but I had no idea how to replicate what they've done with Waldo's Diner."

Carson nodded. "Since Chester and Karen wanted to retire, there was no way for Callie to work under them as a waitress either."

Callie bit her lip. "So Carson asked them if they'd be willing to open Waldo's Diner so I could train under them for a year and eventually buy or rent it from them."

My jaw dropped. "You want to run the restaurant?" I'd never thought about it, but the idea made complete sense.

Rory said, "You'd be amazing at that, Callie!"

Jordan nodded in agreement. "It's almost like how your parents always made us feel so welcome here. You'd be continuing the tradition."

Zara added, "And there's so much opportunity

for growth. You could do courses on running a good restaurant, franchise, have merch."

Kai said, "I could help you design an app too. Make sure the diner's up-to-date technologically speaking."

Callie seemed stunned at our reaction. "You guys are all okay with it?"

Beckett asked, "Why wouldn't we be?"

"Because we all worked so hard to bring Waldo's Diner back for Chester and Karen. I didn't want you all to feel like I was profiting from all your hard work."

Ronan replied, "We worked so hard because we loved what Chester and Karen created. I think anyone would be happy for their tradition to be carried on, especially if you're going to learn from them how to do it the right way."

Carson rubbed his wife's shoulder. "See, babe? I told you they'd love this."

My eyes were watering again with tears of joy. It had been so defeating to work on the documentary and see the community rally around the diner, just to have it stop once we reached our savings goal. "So Waldo's Diner is back on?"

Cori grinned. "We can go ahead with the offer. I just need to approve the land inspection to move forward. We'll be able to close quickly, since we're buying with cash. It will be in Chester and Karen's name."

Zara said, "Let's do it! We need to celebrate!"

"How about when Carson gets back from North Carolina?" I asked. "I want Ray to be here for the party too."

"Sounds good," Callie said.

We stayed and talked for a little while, but it was getting dark, so I had to excuse myself. Ray always went to bed early since he always woke at dawn to feed the cattle, and I knew he'd wait up for me if I stayed out.

I got in my car and started driving back toward the farm, a true-crime podcast blasting through the speakers. I probably shouldn't have been grinning this big with murder details going on in the background, but I couldn't help it.

Life was as good as it had ever been.

But then a deer jumped in front of my car. I slammed on my breaks, but not soon enough. The animal crashed into my hood, rolling up over the vehicle. Then another one crashed into the window on the driver's side.

At shattering glass, I jerked my wheel away from the impact, and my vehicle rolled through the air.

TWENTY-SEVEN

RAY

I YAWNED and glanced at the clock on my phone. It was past ten o'clock. I usually went to bed at nine, but I wanted to make sure Ginger got home safe. I knew she'd probably be fine, but it didn't feel right going to sleep without her. So I pushed play on another episode of *The Ranch* and sat back on the couch.

My phone rang, her name on the screen. I grinned, tapping to answer, and held it up to my ear. "I was just thinking about you."

"Ray?"

The shake in her voice made my heart stop. "What happened?" Adrenaline filled my body and I jumped up from the couch, already walking to the door.

"I was in an accident." Her voice was constricted.

"Are you okay? What kind of accident?"

"I rolled the car." Her voice shook. "A deer hit the side of the car, and I know you always say not to overcorrect, but I panicked and jerked the wheel and—"

I was already out the door, getting into my pickup. "Baby, you didn't do anything wrong. Are you *hurt*? Did you call an ambulance?"

"They said they're on the way."

"Are you hurt?" I repeated, desperation filling my voice.

"I—I don't know. I'm bleeding. I don't think anything's broken. The car's totaled. I'm so sorry."

"I don't give a shit about the car," I said, flying out of the driveway. "I care about *you*. Do you know where you are?"

"I'm just outside of Heywood."

"Is anyone with you?"

"No one's driven by yet, I don't think."

"Are you in the car?"

"The dispatcher said I should climb out the window if I was able... in case the car exploded."

I swore under my breath and wiped at the tears leaking from my eyes. Ginger could have died tonight, and I was here, away from the love of my life. "I'll be there in less than ten minutes."

"Thank you," she whispered.

"Can you see any headlights down the road?" I asked as I gunned it as fast as was safe down the dirt road. I hated the thought of her sitting in the ditch by herself.

"Not yet." Her voice shook. "It's cold out here at night."

I tightened my grip on the wheel, hoping like hell it wasn't shock setting in. "It is cold."

Sirens blared in the background of her phone. "That must be the ambulance. I can see lights flashing."

"That's good, baby. They'll be able to get a good look at you, bring you to the hospital to get you checked out." I pushed the truck harder, dust billowing behind me in the taillights. I needed to be there for her. See her with my own two eyes.

"Where are you?" she asked.

"I'm still about five minutes away."

The sirens grew louder. "They're here," she said. "I should talk to them."

"I'll be there in two minutes," I promised. "I love you, Ginger."

"I love you too," she said, and the call ended.

The next two minutes were the longest of my life. I prayed out loud that she'd be okay. That there wouldn't be any lasting harm done to her from the accident. That we'd get her checked out at the hospital and then I could hold her close all night.

And then I saw the ambulance lights in the distance. My heart constricted at the sight of her car, all mangled metal and broken glass. At the sight of the dead animal on the side of the road, blood spilled on the dirt.

I got out of the truck, running to the ambulance, where an EMT was closing the door.

"That's my wife!" I shouted.

The guy turned to me, opening the door. Good thing too because no amount of force could have kept me from her. I climbed into the back of the ambulance, seeing her lying on the gurney, belted in. Her red hair was a matted mess around her, and there were cuts bleeding on her face, her arms that weren't covered by a blanket.

"Baby," I said, getting close and taking her in.

She reached for me, pulling me to her bleeding lips, and I kissed her gently. "What's going on?"

An EMT answered for me, shutting the door as the ambulance began to drive. "She has several deep cuts that will need stitches. Her left arm and ankle are tender, but we'll need an X-ray to see if there are any breaks. She's lucky to be alive."

Fear released from my eyes, trailing tears down my cheeks. "Baby, I'm here. I'm here." It was all I could do. I couldn't go back and drive her myself. Couldn't tell her to take my truck instead of the car.

I tried to shove those thoughts down, the ones that told me I should have done better. She was here, and that's what we needed to focus on.

They brought us to the ER, and the nurses began a flurry of activities, asking us all kinds of questions, from her birthday to her allergies. Ginger answered them robotically, and I couldn't take my eyes off her for fear something would change.

They cut all her clothes off since her left side was so tender, and I could see bruises blossoming on her fair skin. The sight of them made me sick, but I swallowed down bile, not wanting to take away from her care for even a second. A nurse drew blood for testing, and I stared at the red liquid coming from her veins. Proof of life, I reminded myself. Proof she would be okay.

A tech took her for X-rays, and when she came back, a doctor began cleaning her wounds, bandaging the shallow ones and stitching two on her arm that were particularly deep and one above her lip. Then he pulled the X-rays onto the screen, examining each one.

"You have a fracture in your left arm," he said. "Your ankle is just badly bruised."

Ginger nodded.

"Since you have stitches on this side, we'll splint it until the swelling goes down and the stitches can be removed, and then we'll have you in a more permanent cast."

"Thank you," she said.

"But everything else is okay?" I asked. "She's going to be okay?"

The doctor nodded. "Considering the accident, she's lucky to be walking out of it at all. In fact, her swerving away from the animal might have saved her completely. If it had gotten into the car through the broken window, the odds would look even worse."

I choked on my emotion, looking down at my girl. My brave, beautiful wife.

"There is one more test we were waiting on," he said. "Let me go check the results."

I nodded, kneeling next to Ginger's bed, brushing her hair back.

She smiled slightly. "You know that extra inhaler you have me keep in the glove compartment? I was starting to have a panic-induced asthma attack, and I used it so I could call 911." She reached up, brushing tears from my cheek with her thumb. "You saved me."

I held her hand to my face, trying not to imagine the million different ways tonight could have gone. "You are so strong, Ginger. Braver than me."

The door opened again, and the doctor came in, holding a chart. "The results to that test came back." He looked between the two of us. "You're pregnant."

TWENTY-EIGHT

ZARA

RONAN and I went to my dad's place for supper Monday night. He had phaal curry delivered, and Ronan was already sweating halfway through the meal. It had been a while since I'd had such a spicy meal, and I enjoyed the richness of the flavors and the burn on my tongue.

Ronan offered to clean the dishes after our meal, and Dad said, "Zara, will you come with me?"

"Sure," I said. "Did you accidently disconnect your smart watch again?"

Dad grumbled about Bluetooth being witchcraft as we went upstairs toward his bedroom. This home wasn't nearly as lavish as the one I'd grown up in, but he had beautiful tall ceilings and a view into open space from French doors to the balcony.

I was so busy taking in the sunset view I almost missed the big white box on his bed. "That's not a watch," I said, gesturing at it.

Dad had a soft smile on his face. "No, it's not."

My eyebrows drew together.

"It's your mother's wedding dress."

My mouth fell open, and I covered it with my hands. "Her dress?" I'd stared at the photo of them on their wedding day a million times over, wishing I could touch the intricate beading or smell her perfume. I thought it had been lost back in India. "How did you find it?"

"Auntie Khatri went through your grandmother's estate for it. She found the dress in storage. It had to be dry cleaned, but it's in amazing condition." He gestured at the box. "Take a look."

My hands shook as I reached for the corners of the box, slowly lifting the cardboard to reveal a cream-colored gown inside. The sash lay atop the dress, half gauze, half fabric with a beaded applique. I ran my fingers over the material, feeling it go from soft and flowy to hard and rigid.

"Your mother was a little larger than you are,

but it can be taken in," he said. "If you want to wear it."

I wiped away tears on my eyes, lifting the skirt of the dress from the box. I held it to my chest, taking in my image reflected in the mirrored closet doors. "Of course I want to wear it," I said. I couldn't think of anything more beautiful, or meaningful, than to have Mom with me on my wedding day in the form of this dress.

Dad had told me it was specially designed for her. I even loved that it was made of two pieces and showed her midriff. It always made me feel like if my mom could be the most beautiful woman on the planet with her tummy bared, then there was nothing holding me back from loving myself out loud.

"I've spoken with our travel agent and a wedding planner in Chennai, and we have a few options for a date. One four months from now, which I know is soon, one fourteen months from now, and one a year and half from now. We can also fly each of your friends and their partners there with us. I know how important they are to you."

"Are you sure, Dad?" I looked down at the wedding dress in my hands. "It's all so much."

He gestured at the bench at the foot of the bed

and sat down on one end. I sat next to him, draping the skirt over my lap. I couldn't take my hands off it —it was like a piece of my mom, carrying her energy in its fibers.

He reached over, covering my hand on the dress. "Six years ago, I tried so hard to find you a match who would provide for you for life. After that failed—miserably—you proved something to me."

I looked up at him, seeing the light shining in his eyes. "What's that?"

"You proved that you could provide for yourself. You've grown our adaptations department very profitably and have helped Bhatta Productions become a company authors dream of working with. You don't need a man, which makes your commitment to Ronan that much more special. You don't have family or financial pressures bringing you two to the altar; it's love. The kind that your mother and I built over years together. I want to celebrate that with you."

Tears fell down my cheeks, and I let them fall, reaching for my dad to hug him close. I only wished that my mom could see us now.

Ronan and I left Dad's house with Mom's dress in the trunk of our car and a box of phaal curry in the back seat. I made a mental note not to forget it in the car because I'd definitely regret that smell for the next few days.

Ronan reached across the console, holding my hand. "What are you thinking for a date?"

I smiled at him. "Tomorrow? Yesterday?"

His chuckle crinkled his eyes at the corners. I realized once again how lucky I was to be with my high school sweetheart. Over the last several years, I'd watched him grow up, seen his body change from wiry and strong to solid and built. His hair had darkened slightly from more time indoors, and the crinkles around his eyes were beginning to settle in faintly. My body had filled out too since high school. Instead of long locks, I'd opted for a chic bob that was easier to care for in the mornings. My flashy, youthful wardrobe had become demure, polished.

I couldn't wait to see where another ten years would take us, couldn't imagine twenty or thirty more with him at my side.

"I'm happy with any of the dates. He planned around our release schedule, so even with a week in India, we should be good with work."

I nodded. "Why don't we double-check with our friends, make sure the date works for them and go that way?"

"I love that plan. Why don't you call them?"

"Now?" I asked.

His smile melted my heart. "You're the one who said you wanted to get married yesterday."

With a laugh, I let go of his hand and got my phone from my purse. A few taps later, and I had a group call sent out to all the girls.

Callie answered first. It looked like she was at a restaurant.

"Are you busy?" I asked her.

"Just dropped Carson off at the airport. Thought I'd grab a bite to eat."

Rory came on the line next, holding her nephew. Then Jordan answered, wearing her white lab coat. They were all saying hello when Ginger answered.

My heart immediately sank, and I covered my mouth. The side of her face was bruised, and she had stitches on her lip, her eyebrow.

"Oh my gosh, Ginger, what happened?"

She looked off camera and then tilted the phone so we could see Ray. His expression was grim as he said, "She had a roll-over accident on the way home last night. We just got home from the hospital."

Ronan sucked in a breath.

"Is anything broken?" I asked.

Ginger said, "My arm is fractured." Her voice was rough and tired.

Callie said, "You don't have to talk, honey. Save your energy. Do you two need anything?"

Ray replied, "Ginger's mom is staying over to help us out, and my mom is just half a mile away, so I think we're covered. Your prayers would mean a lot though, because..."

He paused as if checking with her.

"Tell them," she whispered.

"Because Ginger's pregnant."

"Oh my gosh," I breathed, seeing my friend in an entirely different light.

Ray's smile was tender. "The doctor said it's early, about six weeks, but he's hopeful they'll both be okay. She'll be on bed rest for the next couple weeks, just to be safe."

My eyes watered for the second time that night. "You're having a baby?"

Ginger smiled, then flinched. "We are."

Rory cleared her throat. "Congratulations, Ging. That's amazing."

Callie said, "You and Ray are going to have the *cutest* babies. Can you imagine a little redheaded girl running around in boots and a cowboy hat?"

Ginger said, "You're making me smile too much. It hurts my lip."

"Sorry," Callie said quickly. "We'll let you rest. And, Ray, you let us know if our girl needs anything, okay?"

"I will," he promised.

The call ended, and I felt shaky. Ginger had been in a car accident. One that had left her battered and bruised, and I was thinking about postponing my wedding? I learned with my mom that none of us was promised tomorrow.

"Ronan?" I said softly.

"Yeah, babe?"

"Let's take the soonest date."

TWENTY-NINE
RORY

I HELD the phone to my chest and glanced at the bathroom door. I could still see little slivers of tape that had been left behind by my ovulation and cycle trackers. My fingers itched to use one of the pregnancy tests I'd bought in bulk, but I shook my head as if I could shake off the urge, the jealousy I felt no matter how happy I wanted to be for her.

"Who was that?" Beckett asked, coming into the room. But his features fell at the sight of me.

"Ginger was in an accident," I sniffed, afraid of letting him see the ugliest parts of me. "And they found out that she's pregnant."

I was an awful friend. Ginger had just gotten home from the hospital after a horrible accident, and I was... jealous. They had just started trying, and already they had a baby on the way. They were probably pregnant before they even really tried. And yet, she already knew the feeling of life growing inside her in a way I'd dreamed of for well over a year. I'd taken medications, changed my diet, tracked my cycles, and it still hadn't happened for us.

"Is the baby okay?" Beckett asked.

I nodded, my throat tight with emotion. "She has to take it easy for the next few weeks, just to be sure."

"How far along?"

"Six weeks," I managed.

In thirty-four weeks, she and Ray would have a baby. A perfect mix of them, hopefully with her spunk and his heart, and most importantly, with two parents who loved him or her beyond belief.

And I had no doubt that I'd be here. My womb, my home, empty.

I knew Beckett and I had to be enough, that we would make it through. But it hurt. Damn, it hurt so much.

Beckett wrapped his arms around me. "Do they need anything? I know I'm leaving tomorrow, but maybe you could bring some freezer meals out there?"

His thoughtfulness brought the tears to the surface. "You're too good for me."

He kept hugging me anyway. "What do you mean?"

I pulled back, wiping at my eyes. "I'm glad Ginger's okay, but I can't stop this jealous feeling that she gets to have a baby and I don't!" I didn't want to see the disappointment in his face, but I couldn't look away. "She just went through something horrible, and all I'm thinking about is my own selfish desires."

I expected him to be repulsed, to tell me how awful I was, but he held my face in his hands. "You can have both, babe."

"What do you mean?" I asked, still not understanding his reaction. Because I felt so gross to myself.

"Of course you're worried about your friend and happy she's okay, and... And. You're dealing with the grief of infertility. It's not convenient, but it's real, Rory. It doesn't make you a bad person, just a real one."

Tears fell down my cheeks, of grief, of relief.

He'd seen me in a way I hadn't been able to see myself. "I am glad she's okay. You should have seen her. She had stitches and bruises on her face. I can't even imagine what the rest of her looked like."

"Poor Ginger... That must have been terrifying for her and Ray."

I nodded. "Especially after he lost his dad so young."

"I couldn't imagine losing you." He kissed the top of my head.

I shook my head, not even wanting to imagine what life would be like without Beckett. I already had a hard time missing him during football season when he had to be gone so much photographing the games.

"Hey." He wiped away my tears with his thumbs. "Why don't we go to the store and get some ingredients. We'll make them some freezer meals, and you can bring them out after work tomorrow. How's that sound?"

"Good." I leaned into his chest, breathing in his scent. Breathing in the smell of home.

I slowed on the dirt road and pulled off to the side, covering my mouth. Ginger's maroon car sat in the empty field, tangled with barbed wire and mangled beyond recognition. All the windows were broken out, and the tires were completely flat.

I choked out a sob, the reality of it all hitting me like one punch after another.

Ginger could have *died*. Judging by her car, that was the more likely outcome. The fact that she and her baby had made it out alive, with only some stitches and a fracture... It was a miracle.

With shaking hands, I pulled back onto the road and carefully drove the rest of the way to her and Ray's house. I recognized her family's van out front, along with Ray's truck and another pickup I didn't recognize. Probably belonged to his mom or one of his siblings.

I got out of my car, taking a deep breath of country air to steady myself. If seeing her car had been that hard in person... I'd have to brace myself to see my sweet friend and handle her with care.

I heard the front door open and looked up to see Ray. He wore sweats and slides, and as he approached me, I realized just how haggard he looked. His scruff grown out, circles under his eyes, and a tightness around his lips.

"Rory, I didn't know you were coming."

"I wanted to bring some freezer meals... I didn't know what else to do."

He hugged me tight. "She'll be glad to see you."

"How is she?" I asked, biting my lip.

"She's strong. Her neck is sore, so she's mostly resting and watching movies. Of course she refuses to take anything but Tylenol because she doesn't want to hurt the baby."

My heart panged for all three of them.

"Come on in. I'll help you carry the food," he said.

We reached into my trunk, each of us holding four pans of food and walking up to the front door. Both their moms sat at the table, sipping from mugs of coffee. Their conversation stalled as I walked in, and they jumped up to help us with the pans.

With the meals out of my hands, Ginger's mom hugged me tight. "Rory, that was so nice of you to bring food over."

"I know you probably had everything handled, but Beckett and I wanted to do something," I admitted.

She patted my back, and Mrs. Sadler said, "Why don't you two go back? I think I just heard the credits on the last show."

Ray nodded, and I followed him to their bedroom. I stalled in the doorway, seeing my friend lying in the bed, her arm propped up on pillows, her stitches and bruises so stark against her pale skin.

"You have a visitor," Ray said.

Ginger turned her head slightly my way, and her lips spread until she flinched. "Rory, you didn't have to come."

"Of course I did," I replied, sitting on the side of her bed opposite her injured arm.

Ray looked between the two of us. "I'm going help Mom get that stuff in the deep freeze. I'll see you in a bit."

He walked back out, leaving just the two of us. My eyes watered as I took her in. "I'm so glad you're okay, Ging."

Her eyes seemed to darken. "It was so scary. One minute, I was listening to a podcast, and the next, everything was different."

I nodded, pushing back images of her damaged car. A swell of nausea came over me, and I held my hand to my mouth, rushing away from her bedside and making acquaintances with her toilet.

I cleaned myself up, carefully wiping down her

toilet and anything I touched with disinfectant wipes.

"You okay?" Ginger called.

"I'm so sorry," I said, standing in the doorway between the bathroom and her bedroom. "I feel better now, but it was just so sudden. But I should probably go. I don't want to get you sick. A stomach bug is the last thing you need right now."

"Unless... never mind."

I drew my eyebrows together. "Unless what?"

"Maybe it's not a stomach bug," she said.

Comprehension dawned, making me raise my eyebrows. "Don't be silly."

"What, have you cycled?"

"No, but I'm not regular."

"Well, you *could* be sick, and you *could* have to go home. But I kind of want someone other than Ray to watch *Clueless* with, so will you take a test just to humor me? I have an extra one in that top drawer by the sink."

I let out a sigh. Under any other condition, I would have told her I'd see her when I got to feeling better. But she looked so hopeful, there in her recovery bed. And watching *Clueless* with her, drooling over Paul Rudd, hearing her breathe and knowing she was okay... that sounded amazing.

So I went back into the bathroom, found a test, and sat on the toilet.

"There," I said. "We'll have results in three minutes." I set the test on the counter and braced myself for the disappointment that always came with only one pink line.

THIRTY

BECKETT

THE TEAM'S private plane landed on the tarmac, and I texted Rory.

Beckett: Just landed. Be home soon.

The great thing about flying with the team was we could use the small private airport in Emerson instead of going all the way to LA to fly in and out of LAX. That meant I could grab my bags and be home in half an hour, and man, did I want to get home.

I missed my girl like crazy during the football season, when the team had to go out of town so often. We texted and video called, but it just wasn't enough. At least this was the last out-of-town spring training game for a little while.

Rory: Can't wait to see you. <3

Beckett: Me neither. Love you. <3

The plane stopped on the tarmac, and the flight attendants let everyone out. We all got our bags delivered to us on the runway, and then cars began approaching to pick everyone up. I rode on the shuttle next to the team's water boys and said goodbye before going to my car.

I lugged my camera gear and travel bag in the trunk and then got in. Even though I was excited to see Rory, I stopped by the supermarket and bought a flower arrangement, some watercolor paints, and a pad of paper, thinking we could paint together tonight. It had been a while since we'd done that, and I wanted to spend time with her. Talk to her. Hear all about how visiting Ginger had gone and how the school week was so far.

They were nearing the end of the year, which meant she'd be busier than usual, helping out with prom, award ceremonies, and graduation. I loved hearing her stories about the students this time of year and remembering what it felt like to be in school again.

Our house came into view, and I smiled at it. Rory had insisted we paint the siding bright yellow the year we moved in, and it always made me happy when I looked at it—even if I'd almost fallen off the roof trying to paint the inoperative chimney.

She had pottery lined along the front of the house, some made by students, some made by her, and some thrifted at stores along the coast. And since neither of us could keep a plant alive, fake flowers and greenery spilled over their edges.

I parked beside Rory's car in the driveway, knowing I'd find her inside. The thought had me leaving my bags in the trunk and just bringing inside the art supplies and flowers.

Before I got to the front door, Rory had it open, wrapping her arms around me and squeezing me tight. I breathed in her sweet floral scent and basked in the warmth of her embrace.

"I missed you," I said.

"Me too," she replied, stepping back and smiling at the bouquet. "You got me flowers?"

"Of course I did." I kissed her cheek and followed her inside, seeing our house looking tidy. "You did some cleaning while I was gone."

"You weren't here to distract me," she teased, smiling up at me. "Set that down. I got us some ice cream."

I grinned. "I'm not sure what's better—coming home to a beautiful girl like you or a dish of ice cream."

She hit my shoulder, and I laughed.

I put the bag of art supplies on the counter and then sat across from her at the table, looking at my bowl of mint chocolate chip ice cream, drizzled in chocolate syrup, the spoon already in place. "And here I thought I was surprising you with something nice."

She smiled. "What did you get?"

"I thought we could do some watercolor tonight? Maybe see if you can show me how to paint the flowers on our lemon tree in the backyard."

"That sounds nice," she said, a twinkle in her eye.

"What?" I asked.

She quickly looked down at her own ice cream. "Nothing. Just happy you're home."

"Sure," I replied with a smile, taking a bite of the ice cream.

She watched me expectantly.

"What?" I asked with my mouth full.

"Nothing!" she said again.

I laughed. "You're acting weird."

"Am I?" She took a bite of her ice cream and stuck out her tongue with a green lump of ice cream sitting atop.

I laughed at her. "Goober."

I took another bite of ice cream, sliding my lips over the cold spoon. Then it was bumpy.

I drew my eyebrows together, checking the spoon to see if something had stuck to it in the dishwasher, when I noticed words engraved into the metal.

You're going to be a daddy.

My jaw dropped, and I looked between the spoon and Rory, whose smile was growing by the second.

"Are you for real?" I asked.

She nodded giddily.

My lips spread into a disbelieving smile. "You're kidding!"

"No, I'm not! I found out on Friday!"

"Tuesday!?" I yelled. "You talked to me for *six days* without spilling the beans?"

She nodded again, getting up from her chair and sitting in my lap. "It was so hard to keep the secret, but I wanted to have a doctor's appointment to be sure." She reached into her front overall pocket and retrieved a black and white image, a little bean-like baby in the middle.

"That's our baby?" I asked, my eyes hot.

She nodded, tears falling down her cheeks. "That's our baby."

WHILE CARSON WAS BACK in North Carolina, packing up our things and finishing out his last two weeks of work, I went all around town looking for new places we could live. Every apartment just seemed so out of reach. With the latest housing boom in California, rent was either too expensive or would be a long distance from the diner.

Today had been my last chance to secure a place before he got into town later tonight, but the tenth apartment tour had been a dud. Carson was working so hard in North Carolina, training his successor during the day and then packing up and cleaning our apartment at night, and yet I had nothing for him back here.

"No luck?" Mom asked.

I jerked my head up, gripping at my heart. "Mom, I didn't see you in the kitchen!"

She gave me a guilty smile, wiping her hand on a towel. "I was decorating some sugar cookies. It's been a while since I've done that. Do you want one?"

I nodded, letting out a sigh.

"What was wrong with this place?" she asked.

"I thought it would be okay, not perfect, but livable... until I saw the cockroaches in the bathroom."

Mom's face pinched. "That's disgusting."

"But bathrooms are kind of gross," I said. "Maybe we could lay traps and deal with it when it happened?" I loved staying with my parents, but a married couple needed their own place. "I just wanted Carson to have something good to come home to, you know?"

"I know you did, honey." Mom carried a plate of cookies decorated like dairy cows to the table. "But there's no way you're staying in a roach infested apartment when you could stay here."

I lifted my lips slightly, taking a cookie and biting off a piece. Mom made the best sugar cookies—they were soft and buttery, full of flavor. "Delicious, Mom."

She smiled. "Thank you. You know, your dad and I have been talking..."

"I know the door's always open," I said. I felt like we had this talk after every failed attempt. "I appreciate it. I really do." But it wasn't fair to Carson to stay here every night, right next door to the place that had given him so much trauma to work through.

"You're right," she said. "But when Joe and Gemma moved back, we helped them with a down payment on their house."

My eyebrows lifted. "I thought Gemma was making good money in New York."

"She was, and they didn't need us to help, but we wanted to take the pressure off their move," Mom said. "You're not a parent yet, but someday you'll understand. It feels good to help your children out from time to time. And now we want to help you and Carson."

"What do you mean?" I asked.

"When he gets a job and you know what type of mortgage you're able to afford, we will make the down payment for you."

My mouth fell open, and I covered it, holding back tears. The relief of having a home, not having to rent some overpriced apartment without so much as a yard... "What did I do to deserve all this, Mom?"

"What do you mean?" she asked, reaching across the table to touch my forearm.

"I mean, the restaurant was a lot and now the house? I feel so lucky... and I've seen so many people who have nothing. What did I do to earn this?"

Mom tilted her head, deep in thought. "You didn't do anything to *earn* your parents' love, just like those kids you worked with didn't deserve bad things to happen to them. It's life, honey. But you can still enjoy the fortunes that come to you—those you work for and those you get just because. Just don't forget to pass it on when you can."

I nodded, determined to make the most of what had been given to me. I'd make sure to carry on Chester's legacy by making Waldo's Diner the most welcoming place in Emerson. I'd make my home a place full of love for my family and someday my children and their friends, just like my parents had.

It might not be the same thing as being a social worker, but I had to believe the love I had for others, in any capacity, would make ripples in the world around me.

A horn beeped outside, and I turned in my seat,

looking out the window. A big moving truck with our car in tow pulled up along the curb. I grinned, feeling like it was the day Carson's family had moved in.

But instead of a ten-year-old boy, a twenty-five-year-old man was stepping onto the lawn. He was tall, lean, and tan. His blond hair had been cut just short enough to look messy when he ran his fingers through it.

And instead of walking toward the house next door, he was walking toward me.

"Carson," I breathed, getting up and running through the front door to meet him.

He grinned when he saw me, and I jumped into his arms. He took a couple steps back before gaining footing and spinning me in a circle. "It's so good to see you, Cal."

I squeezed him even tighter. "I thought you weren't getting in until later tonight!" I kissed him and then pulled back, waiting for his explanation.

"Our neighbor helped me carry some things down to the truck, so it went way faster than I thought it would. Hope you don't mind the surprise."

I'd been on the verge of tears earlier, and now

they streamed easily down my cheeks. "Of course I don't mind."

He set me down, thumbing away my tears. "I didn't think you'd be crying when I came home."

"It's been a hard day," I admitted. We stood in the front yard while I explained the latest apartment failure, and my mom's news.

His jaw dropped open. "Cal, you're not going to believe this, but on the way here, I got a call from Birdie."

I covered my mouth. "No."

He nodded. "I'm the new gym teacher at Emerson Academy's elementary school, Callie. I have a job. We're going to have a *home!*" He picked me up again, swinging me around.

I thought I knew what happiness felt like—I knew it in a girls' night with my friends or a hug from my parents or the way Carson looked at me like I was the only girl in the world.

But this feeling? This flying, soaring feeling full of possibility? It was so much more than I'd ever felt before, and I couldn't wait to see what was to come with Carson at my side.

MY MOM TURNED AWAY from the mirror in the hotel's dressing room and faced me in her beautiful cream dress. The top was solid with long sleeves and a beaded waist that connected to a flowing tulle skirt that clung loosely to her hips and thighs.

The dress wasn't designed to hide any part of her, but to show her off.

"Ama," I breathed. "You look beautiful."

She smiled, pressing at the corners of her eyes. "I never thought I would get married again."

"I hoped you would," I admitted.

"You did?" She stepped down from the podium, holding my hand as she walked us to the seating area. Arabella had gone to the bathroom, so it was just the two of us in this beautiful space.

I nodded. "It wasn't fair of you to be alone through all of that. You deserved a good partner, one who could see how amazing you are." Part of me wondered if Javier was good enough for her, but Mom was happy, and that was all that mattered.

She smiled. "I always felt like you were the love of my life, Jordan."

And now I was crying. "Mom."

"It has been the best gift of my life to watch you grow and turn into the woman you are now."

I wrapped my arms around her, holding her tight, remembering when it was just the two of us in that tiny one-bedroom apartment. We'd both come so far.

The door opened, and we pulled away, looking toward the door. Arabella came in, wearing her version of our bridesmaid dress.

"Hey, Bella," Mom said.

Arabella seemed a little uncomfortable, fidgeting with a box in her hands. "Um, Jordan, Jacinda, Dad wanted me to give these to you."

Curious what he could have to give me, I took the box from her. It was flat and long, charcoal black with a satin purple ribbon holding it together. Mom and I exchanged a glance, and then I looked down to my gift, slowly pulling off the ribbon.

When I lifted the box, I first saw a folded sheet of paper with the impressions of an ink pen ghosting through the page. Pulling the sheet out revealed a golden necklace with two linked hearts on the end.

I glanced up at Mom, her eyes red as they traveled the words on the page.

I unfolded my own letter and looked down at his handwriting, my vision quickly blurring.

Dear Jordan,

When I first met your mother, I was enamored with her beauty, inspired by her success, and in awe of her humility. But one of the things that quickly made me fall was her love and commitment to you. I knew a woman so fiercely dedicated to her daughter was a woman of integrity, one who could build a relationship that lasts.

Although you and I don't know each other as well as I'd like, I feel like I know you as well as my own daughter by the way Jacinda speaks of you. Through her stories, I know you're smart as a whip, just as hard-working as your mother, and that when you love, whether it's family or friends, you love with your whole heart.

I hope you'll take this necklace as a symbol of my understanding that you and your mother are a package deal. I'd never dream of marrying her without thinking of you as part of the family, forever and ever.

I promise to work to make both of you feel loved, starting today and every day for the rest of my life.

Love,

Javier

I sniffed, wiping at my eyes, and pulled out the necklace. I was planning to ask my mom to help me put it on, but Arabella said, "Can I help?"

Smiling gently, I nodded. "That would be great."

She took the necklace from my hands, and I lifted my hair as she clasped it at the back of my neck. Stepping back, she looked at me and said, "V cute, Jordan."

I'd been around enough teens in the hospital to know it meant very cute. "Thank you," I said, smiling.

Mom came to us, putting her arms around the both of us. Arabella giggled, making me laugh too.

"I love you girls," Mom said.

"Love you, Mom."

"You're the best, Jacinda," Arabella said. "I'm glad my dad chose you."

Mom started crying all over again.

We helped her touch up her makeup, and then the wedding planner was there, telling us it was time.

We walked in a line to the ballroom, beautifully decorated for the ceremony. As the piano played softly, Arabella walked into the aisle.

I gave Mom one last kiss and hug before turning and walking down the aisle. I instantly spotted Kai, smiling at me from the second row. But then I saw who was sitting beside him—all my friends and their men, looking beautiful all dressed up.

I'd been so worried about losing my mom, losing my family, but all this time I hadn't realized what I already had. A family, not from blood, but from bonds so close we could never let go, no matter how many years and miles and obligations had existed between us.

They were my family, too, and they weren't going anywhere.

THIRTY-THREE
GINGER

I HELD my hand over the baby growing in my belly as Ray and I walked into the office of my new ob-gyn. This was the week we'd get to see our child for the first time, and I was so worried and excited I was on the verge of tears to laughter from one minute to the next.

Ray put his large hand on my lower back, steadying me, reminding me that he was there for me. That we were in this together.

The nurse asked me to change so they could do the ultrasound and then left, saying the doctor would be a few minutes. Ray sat down while I shimmied out of my jeans. The look in his eyes was nothing short of steamy.

With my cheeks warm, I said, "Stop looking at me like that, or we'll have twins."

Chuckling, he replied, "That's not how it works."

I shook my head at him, sitting back on the exam table and covering my waist with the sheet the nurse gave me. "Aren't you nervous?"

He tilted his head thoughtfully. "I can't let it eat me."

"What do you mean?"

"If I think about all the bad things that could happen, I wouldn't be able to get up and walk. Much less enjoy this moment with you." His lips softened into a smile. "We're about to see our baby for the first time."

There were the tears. The happy tears. "We're about to see our baby for the first time," I echoed.

He reached across the space between us and held my hand. "Have I mentioned you're going to be a great mom?"

I squeezed his hand. "I can't wait to see you be a dad."

I only wished that his dad could be here to see it. Times like these, I could see a sadness in Ray's eyes. And I knew him well enough to know what it was. Since his dad died his freshman year of high school, he'd missed so many moments—Ray's graduation, our wedding, and now his first grandchild.

A knock sounded on the door, and the ob-gyn, Dr. Dart, walked inside. She had pretty blond hair and thick glasses over hazel eyes. "Hi, you two!" She smiled at us. "Ready to see your baby?"

Ray let go of my hand, and I nodded enthusiastically.

"How have you been feeling?" she asked. "Has the bed rest been okay?"

I nodded. Spending the last few weeks laid up wasn't my favorite thing, but it also gave me time to watch my favorite movies. To go back through old videos I'd taken but hadn't had time to edit together. And I had time to think—about the kind of mom I wanted to be.

"Any morning sickness?" she asked.

I shook my head. "Only a couple of days in the morning. I think I'm just really lucky. That and my mom gave me these ginger pops that are really supposed to help."

"That is lucky," she replied. "Any unusual pains?"

I shook my head. "A lot of the soreness from the accident has gone away too. What are the chances —" My throat felt tight. "What are the odds that the baby..." I couldn't bring myself to speak another word.

Dr. Dart's eyes were tender. "Let's just take a look."

She had me sit back on the exam table and put my feet in the stirrups. I clenched my jaw and stared at the screen as the black and white image shifted.

Ray came beside me, holding my hand tightly in both of his.

Ever so slowly, the picture came into focus, and I covered my mouth with my free hand.

There on the screen, despite every odd, was our tiny little baby.

"There it is," Dr. Dart said, smiling.

Ray leaned in, dropping a kiss on my forehead.

I tore my gaze away from the screen to look at him, and my voice was hoarse as I breathed. "Our baby."

He kissed me. "Our baby."

THIRTY-FOUR
ZARA

RONAN and I pulled up to the wreckage site of Waldo's Diner. I could see a couple of news vans parked along the street, there to publicize the official groundbreaking for the rebuild of Waldo's Diner.

It had been a long couple of months between work, meeting with the travel planner for our wedding, helping Callie and Carson move into their new home, and visiting Ginger while she was on bed rest. But I was excited to see this project through.

The blueprints for the diner looked incredible—a perfect mix of honoring its history while expanding it slightly to make room for a private party area as well as more seating for guests. They were even adding an outdoor patio to make the most of the great California weather.

It made me think of myself—of all the times I'd thought I'd been broken down completely. I'd always surprised myself by coming back stronger, better, wiser than ever before.

Ronan squeezed my hand. "Excited?"

I nodded. "This is a big moment. I can't believe it's already here."

He got out of the car and came around to open my door for me. When I stepped out, I noticed Carson walking toward us from their car.

"Hey, you," he said, giving me a bear hug and then Ronan a hug as well.

"Hey, coach," Ronan teased. "Where's the whistle?"

"Left it at work." Carson winked.

I laughed. I never thought of Carson as a gym teacher, but from everything I'd heard, he was a natural. "Where are we gathering?"

He gestured toward the back side of the diner where all the footage had come from the night of it burning down. We began walking that way together, and behind the charred skeleton of the diner, I saw the rest of our friends. Both Ginger and Rory had the beginnings of adorable baby bumps. Callie looked cute in her black skirt with a denim shirt knotted at her waist. And Jordan had her curls pulled atop her head, looking less stressed than I'd seen her in a long time. Her diamond ring glinted from her hand that wasn't holding Kai's.

Callie glanced our way, grinning at us and her husband. "You're here!" She hurried over and wrapped us in a hug. Then a guy I recognized from the construction company walked behind her, handing out white hard hats. "For the photos," he said.

I grinned, putting it atop my head. Then I turned to Ronan. "Does it go with my outfit?"

He laughed. "You could have a paper bag on your head and it would be trending by tomorrow."

I smiled at him, reaching up to brush his cheek with my thumb. He looked adorable with that white hat contrasting his dark clothes. I bit my lip and got on my tiptoes to whisper in his ear, "I think I might have a new fantasy to play out later."

He chuckled slightly, then bent to kiss me softly. "Same."

We linked hands and went with the rest of our friends, along with Chester and Karen.

"Who should hold shovels?" the man asked, now holding several spades instead of construction hats.

Beckett spoke up, "The girls should be the ones."

Chester nodded in agreement. "We wouldn't be here without them."

My eyes began to water as my heart felt fuller than ever. The man passed each of us a shovel. The tool was heavy in my hands as I walked toward the front of the group with my girls. They posed the five of us in front of the rubble, and I looked at my best friends for a moment. Each of them so different than the girls they were in high school, but at the same time... my family.

Our husbands, fiancés, stood behind the cameraman, and we smiled for every photo. Because we all knew, a friendship like ours could change the world.

Sɪx Mᴏɴᴛʜs Lᴀᴛᴇʀ

I STARED up at the diner through the car's windshield, taking in the curved letters of the sign that said Waldo's Diner. The yellow banner with thick black letters that said **GRAND RE-OPENING.**

The diner was the same color on the outside, chrome, with big windows. But there was also a new patio out front with metal tables positioned around. Inside the restaurant, I could see Callie and Carson, her parents, Chester and Karen, Kai and Jordan.

Beckett said, "Can you believe it?"

I shook my head, already feeling tears sliding down my cheeks. "It's incredible."

He smiled over at me, his hair falling over his eyebrows. "It wouldn't be here without you."

I reached up and brushed his hair back. "I may have gotten it started, but I never could have done all of this alone."

Our baby cooed from the back seat, and I turned smiling at her in the mirror. "Ava, are you ready to get out?"

She made another sweet sound, and I said, "I'll get her."

Honestly, it was one of my favorite things to do, unbuckling her car seat and pulling her into my arms. After spending so long waiting to hold her, she hardly ever passed any time in the carrier unless we were actually in the car.

While Beckett got the baby bag, I pulled her to me, all ten pounds of her according to the last checkup. She'd weighed seven pounds, eight ounces when she was born just a month ago. It was already going by so quickly.

I bent my head to press my lips to her soft brown hair and breathed in.

"Are you sniffing Ava again?" Beckett asked.

I gave him a look, and he cracked a smile.

"It's the best smell, isn't it?" he asked.

"It totally is," I agreed with a grin.

As we began walking to the front, a truck pulled up, and Ginger waved happily at us through the windshield. We waited as they parked and got baby Annie out of the car—short for Anise so they could keep Ginger's family tradition going.

Annie had less hair than Ava, but it was bright red and so adorable. While Ginger carried Annie, Ray held up the bag in solidarity with Beckett. "We've been demoted from hand-holding to pack mules," he said.

Beckett chuckled. "I'll take that over childbirth any day."

Ray shuddered.

"Seriously," Ginger said. "For someone who's been around farm animals his whole life, you wouldn't expect it to get to him."

I swore I saw Ray blush as he held the door open for us.

Just as we got inside, I heard Zara yell, "Coming!"

I turned in the entrance to watch her come in, fabulously dressed as always. Knowing I probably had spit up somewhere on my body, I lived vicariously through her glamour. "You look great, Zara!" I said.

She smiled, giving me a hug around Ava and then hugging Ginger too.

From farther in the diner, Callie called, "Now that everyone's here, the pre-opening party can officially begin! But first, I have a surprise for all the girls."

"Ava's included," I said to Beckett teasingly. It was fun to let him know he was outnumbered nowadays.

We walked up the aisle between seats toward the big booth where the five of us always used to sit. Callie stood in front of it with her hands folded over her chest. "What do you all think?"

Jordan said, "It's amazing, Callie." She looked at the three of us who had just come in. "You'll have to look at all the decorations. They're so thoughtful."

Callie bit her lip. "There's one I hadn't shown you all yet."

Jordan raised her eyebrows, and we all waited for her to explain. She stepped away from the table and gestured at a golden plaque with words embossed inside.

Reserved for the Curvy Girl Club.

I leaned my cheek against Ava's head, ready to cry all over again. And then I looked up over the table and saw a frame holding two photos. One of us in high school, all circled around this table. And another of us, all in our hard hats the day of the groundbreaking. "It's amazing, Callie," I breathed.

She smiled at all of us, wiping at tears falling down her cheeks. "I can't tell you what you all have done for me. Starting all the way back in high school to now, bringing back something that will become my livelihood. I know it's my purpose, and I wouldn't have been able to do it without you.

Jordan put her arm around Callie's shoulders. "We're here for you."

Zara nodded. "We always will be."

"Always," I said, glancing over my shoulder at Beckett. At our families who had come to celebrate with us. We were all so lucky to have each other and to have this place to share. "And to think, it all started with a bet."

Thank you so much for reading The Curvy Girl Club: All Grown Up! I had so much fun writing this story and made some bonus content to inspire me along the way! If you want to see it all (including the note Ray wrote Ginger before their wedding), you can **get it here.**

You can also get the next five books in the Curvy Girl Club at my site for 20% off! <3

BONUS CONTENT!

Access all the bonus content for the Curvy Girl
Club using this QR code!

As I wrote the final words of this story I felt... this overwhelming sense of warmth. Like this was exactly where these girls were meant to end their journey and I was meant to be writing these moments.

I published Rory's story in the heart of the pandemic, and while I hoped it would do well, I never realized just how much it would mean. Since releasing Curvy Girls Can't Date Quarterbacks, I've gotten so many messages from women just like me who found more than entertainment in these stories; they found an escape, a sense of self love, validation for the pain in their past, and a safe place within the pages.

But those effects didn't come from a glamorous,

perfect place. I was a busy mom, working full time, squeezing in all the writing I could during my lunch breaks and a couple evenings a week in a coffee shop.

It would have been easy to look at myself and say, "I'll never write a series that makes an impact. I don't have enough money or time or an audience or a big publisher to put my book in stores." It was harder to understand, at the time, the power of a universal message: you deserve to be loved, exactly as you are.

Now, I know how strong those words are. I've seen how a simple belief can transcend location or nationality or age to bring together some of the most incredible women I've ever met, either in person or online. Some of you believed so much in the Curvy Girl Club, you supported me and this story through the Stelting Stan Membership.

Incredible.

Everyone reading this book is part of a movement. One that says self-love isn't a trend or wishful thinking or belongs only to those with traditional standards of beauty: it's deserved. You deserve to see self-love in fiction and experience it in real life.

I hope you know how powerful that is, and with that belief, you can accomplish anything you desire.

In a lot of ways, we're all like the girls staring at the ashes of Waldo's Diner and knowing something has to change but not being sure how to start or if our efforts will be enough.

I hope you'll take that first step, because I know, firsthand, how amazing the journey can be.

The Curvy Girl Club

Curvy Girls Can't Date Quarterbacks

Curvy Girls Can't Date Billionaires

Curvy Girls Can't Date Cowboys

Curvy Girls Can't Date Bad Boys

Curvy Girls Can't Date Best Friends

Curvy Girls Can't Date Bullies

Curvy Girls Can't Dance

Curvy Girls Can't Date Soldiers

Curvy Girls Can't Date Princes

Curvy Girls Can't Date Rock Stars

Curvy Girls Can't Date Surfers

Curvy Girls Can't Date Curvy Girls (Pride Edition)

The Texas High Series

Chasing Skye

Becoming Skye

Loving Skye

Always Anika

New at Texas High

Abi and the Boy Next Door

Abi and the Boy Who Lied

Abi and the Boy She Loves

The Pen Pal Romance Series

Dear Adam

Fabio Vs. the Friend Zone

Sincerely Cinderella

The Sweet Water High Series: A Multi-Author Collaboration

Road Trip with the Enemy: A Sweet Standalone Romance

YA Contemporary Romance Anthologies

The Art of Taking Chances

Two More Days

Nonfiction

Raising the West

ACKNOWLEDGMENTS

So many people came together to support this project through the Stelting Stans Membership. This book wouldn't be here without you. Thank you for betting on this story and supporting the Curvy Girl Club. You are absolutely incredible and so so appreciated.

Thank you to my husband and children who supported me in writing this story. I spent about a year writing one chapter a week on Sundays, and they always made space for me to do that.

Thanks to Team Kelsie who help make my writing world go 'round! Sally and Annie, you're the dream team. I love you both!

Tricia Harden, you've been my editor from the start of the Curvy Girl Club. Growing something like this with your help and feedback has been nothing short of amazing. Thank you for taking this journey with me!

Courtney Encheff, thank you for narrating this story! I love working with you and hearing your sweet voice bring my words to life! Dakota Hoss, thank you for editing my author's notes so my readers can hear the words in my voice! I love working with you.

Najla Qamber, thank you for creating the most beautiful covers for me and giving me so many options. I appreciate your dedication to these books and making sure they have a lovely package to match!

Thank you to every single person who picked up a book in the Curvy Girl Club. You made me feel heard and seen in a way I never did before. You made dreams come true.

GLOSSARY

Latin Phrases

Ad Meliora: School motto meaning "toward better things."
Audentes fortuna iuvat: Motto of *Dulce Periculum* meaning "Fortune favors the bold."
Dulce Periculum: means "danger is sweet" - local secret club that performs stunts
Multum in Parvo: means "much in little"

Locations

Town Name: Emerson
Location: Halfway between Los Angeles and San Francisco

Surrounding towns: Brentwood, Seaton, Heywood

Emerson Academy: Private school Rory and Beckett attend

Brentwood Academy: Rival private school

Walden Island: Tourism island off the coast, only accessible by helicopter or ferry

Laughlin: Small country between England and Scotland formed in the early 1900s.

MacColl: Capital city of Laughlin where the royal family resides.

MAIN HANGOUTS

Emerson Elementary Library: Where Rory tutors Anna, open to students K-7

Emerson Field: Massive park in the center of Emerson

Emerson Memorial: Local hospital

Emerson Shoppes: Shopping mall

Emerson Trails: Hiking trails in Emerson, near Emerson Field

Halfway Café: Expensive dining option in Emerson, frequented by celebrities

La La Pictures: Movie theater in Emerson

Ripe: Major health food store serving the tri-city area

Roasted: Popular coffee shop in Emerson

JJ Cleaning: Cleaning service owned by Jordan's mom

Seaton Bakery: Delicious dining and drink option in Seaton where Beckett works

Seaton Beach: Beach near Seaton – rougher than the beach near Brentwood

Seaton Pier: Fishing pier near Seaton

Spike's: Local 18-and-under club

Waldo's Diner: local diner, especially popular after sporting events

Apps

Rush+: Game app designed by Kai Rush and his father

Sermo: chat app used by private school students

Important Entities

Bhatta Productions: Production company owned by Zara's father

Brentwood Badgers: Professional football team

Heywood Market: Big ranch/distributor where everyone can purchase their meat locally

Invisible Mountains: Local major nonprofit - Callie's dad is the CEO

Dugan Industries: Owns and manages Brentwood Marina, along with other entities. Owned by Ryker Dugan's father, Trent Dugan.

ABOUT THE AUTHOR

Kelsie Stelting is a body positive romance author who writes love stories with strong characters, deep feelings, and happy endings.

She currently lives in Colorado with her family. You can often find her writing, spending time with family, and soaking up too much sun wherever she can find it.

Visit www.kelsiestelting.com to get a free story and sign up for her readers' group!

facebook.com/kelsiesteltingcreative
twitter.com/kelsiestelting
instagram.com/kelsiestelting

www.ingramcontent.com/pod-product-compliance
Lightning Source LLC
Chambersburg PA
CBHW061524210726
48287CB00006B/1821